Praise for Cathryn Fox's
His Obsession Next Door

"An entertaining plot, sweet yet steamy love story, and a little bit of angst and forgiveness made *His Obsession Next Door* another excellent story by author Cathryn Fox."

~ *Guilty Pleasures Book Reviews*

"Wow, a truly great read! This is a heartwarming, steamy love story that will cause all your senses to remain on high alert. Ms. Fox is an excellent storyteller and her words kept me captivated from start to finish."

~ *Harlequin Junkie*

"Sweet, teasing book. I want to read more, haven't looked into it yet, so don't know when the next book will be released. Just hope that it will be soon."

~ *Confessions from Romaholics*

"The sexual tension between the two was well written and you could just feel it as you read the book, they had great chemistry! The love scenes were well written and just the right amount of hot!"

~ *We Love Kink Reviews*

Look for these titles by
Cathryn Fox

Now Available:

His Obsession Next Door

Cathryn Fox

SAMHAIN
PUBLISHING

Samhain Publishing, Ltd.
11821 Mason Montgomery Road, 4B
Cincinnati, OH 45249
www.samhainpublishing.com

His Obsession Next Door
Copyright © 2014 by Cathryn Fox
Print ISBN: 978-1-61922-675-3
Digital ISBN: 978-1-61921-977-9

Editing by Tera Cuskaden
Cover by Angela Waters

His Obsession Next Door, ISBN 978-1-61921-977-9
First Samhain Publishing, Ltd. electronic publication: February 2014
His Strings to Pull, ISBN 978-1-61922-587-9
First Samhain Publishing, Ltd. electronic publication: October 2014
First Samhain Publishing, Ltd. print publication: July 2015

Dedication

To my faithful Lab, Jersey...always my protector. And to all the military working dogs who help keep us safe.

Chapter One

"What's gotten into the puppies tonight?" Veterinarian Gemma Matthews asked her assistant as she finished securing the last howling pooch into its kennel.

Victoria gave a mock shiver and shot a nervous glance toward the shelter window. "It's the moon. It'll be full tomorrow night."

Despite the uneasy feeling mushrooming inside Gemma, she laughed at her assistant and followed the long column of silver moonlight illuminating a path along the cement floor. She reached the front lobby of her clinic, now eerily quiet after a demanding day of surgeries, and turned to Victoria. She gave a playful roll of her eyes, and said, "You've seen too many scary movies."

Victoria dabbed gloss to her lips, smacked them together and countered with, "Hey, it could happen."

Gemma arched a brow, humoring the young girl she'd hired straight out of veterinary college. "You think?"

"Sure." Victoria's long, blonde ponytail flicked over her shoulder as she gestured to the no-kill shelter attached to the clinic. "That's why the dogs are barking." Her green eyes widened and her voice sounded conspiratorial when she added, "They can sense the big, bad wolf out there, ready to shred a human's heart into a million tiny pieces."

Labrador Retriever bundled in his arms. "Follow me." Jumping into action she turned and found Victoria rushing down the hall toward Exam Room 1, already a step ahead of them.

Gemma moved with haste and worked to quiet her racing heart. "Tell me exactly what happened." She kept her tone low and her voice controlled in an effort to calm Cole and minimize his anxiety.

Keeping pace, he followed close behind her, his feet tight on her heels. "We were out for a run in Sherwood Park," he began. "A squirrel sidetracked him, and he veered off the beaten path. He was jumping a log and didn't see the sharp branch sticking up."

She stole a quick glance over her shoulder and when dark, intense eyes focused on hers, her stomach clenched. "It's going to be okay, Cole. I promise." She drew a breath and gave a silent prayer that it was a promise she could keep. Gemma pushed through the swinging door and gestured with a quick nod toward the sterile examination table while she hurried to ready herself.

Understanding her silent command, Cole secured the whimpering dog onto the prep counter. Gemma's heart pinched when he placed a solid, comforting hand on the animal's head and spoke in soothing tones while Victoria went to work on preparing the pre-surgical sedative.

Gemma scrubbed in quickly and put on her surgery gear. She gave the dog a once-over before she dabbed at the blood to assess the depth of the wound. Angling her head, she cast Cole a quick glance. "Why don't you take a seat in the other room. This could take a while."

"I'm staying," Cole said firmly, their gazes colliding in that old familiar battle of wills.

Uncomfortable with the idea of him watching while she worked, and fully aware that he was a distraction she didn't need during surgery, she urged, "It could get messy."

"I've seen blood before, Gemma." With his feet rooted solidly, he folded his arms across his chest. "I'm not leaving him."

"Cole—"

"I'm fine."

Not wanting to waste time with a debate and knowing Cole was a bomb expert who'd seen his fair share of blood in the field, she gestured toward the chair in the corner. Once Cole stepped away, she cleansed the animal's wounds and continued her assessment.

She checked temperature, pulse and respiration before evaluating Charlie's gums. She shot Victoria a look as her assistant secured the blood pressure cuff and waited for the go ahead on the pre-surgical sedative.

"He's already trying to crash," Gemma said. "We have to go straight to surgery."

Working quickly, Gemma hooked the dog to an I.V. catheter and induced anesthesia while Victoria began the three-scrub process to shave and sterilize Charlie's skin.

Once the dog was clipped and scrubbed, Gemma reassessed. "He's lost a lot of blood, but I'm not seeing any visible organ damage. We'll have to flush the cavity to clean out the debris before we stitch."

As Gemma sprayed the area with warm saline, Victoria called out, "Pulse ox dropping, heart rate down to forty-five."

Damn, this was not good. Fearing she was missing something, she sprayed the area again and gave the cavity another assessment. That's when she noticed the tree had nicked a vessel on the liver. Gemma's heart leaped and worry moved through her as she exchanged a look with Victoria. Keeping her fingers steady and her face expressionless for Cole's sake, she worked quickly to tie the vessel off before it was too late. Once complete, she rinsed the area, and when the bleeding came to a halt, she exhaled a relieved breath.

She turned her attention to her suture. A long while later she glanced at the clock, noting that more than an hour had passed since Cole had first stepped foot in her door. Gemma secured the last stitch, wiped her brow and stood back to examine the dog.

"Vitals are good," Victoria informed her. Gemma gave a nod and took off her surgery garb. She quickly washed up and let loose a slow breath, confident that the dog would recover.

"Will he be okay?" Cole whispered.

Gemma's skin came alive, Cole's soft, familiar voice sending an unexpected curl of heat through her tired body. She turned to him and he stepped closer, the warmth of his body reaching out to her and overwhelming all her senses. As he looked at her with dark, perceptive eyes that knew far too many of her childhood secrets, she jerked her head to the right. "Let's go into the other room."

She pushed through the surgery doors and Cole followed her into the lobby where she could put a measure of distance between them.

"Is Charlie going to be okay?" Cole asked again, raking his hands through short, dark hair that had been cut to military standards.

Gemma rubbed her temples and leaned against the receptionist's counter. "He's lucky you got him to me when you did."

For the first time since stepping into her clinic, his shoulders relaxed slightly. "He's going to be okay?"

"Yes. He's going to be fine." She drew a breath and stared at the man before her, hardly able to believe that he was here in her clinic. Shortly after her botched seduction some ten years ago he'd enlisted in the army and had gone out of his way to avoid her.

As she considered that further, she decided to brave the question that had been plaguing her since he'd darkened her doorway. She waved her hand around the front lobby. "Why did you bring him here? There are other clinics closer to Sherwood Park."

Silence lingered for a minute, then in a voice that was too quiet, too careful, he said, "Because you were here, Gems, and I wouldn't trust Charlie's care in anyone else's hands but yours."

Her throat tightened at the use of his nickname for her, and while her heart clenched, touched at the level of trust he had in her, her brain cells made the next logical leap. "You've been back for a while, then," she stated in whispered words.

An expression she couldn't quite identify flitted across his face as he said, "A week now."

"Oh." Gemma shifted slightly, trying not to feel wounded that he'd been home for seven long days and hadn't even bothered to say hello.

She averted her gaze to shield the hurt but when he added, "I wanted to come sooner," she knew she could never hide anything from him.

She held her hand up to cut him off. "I understand how difficult this must be for you," she assured him, her mind going back to the last time they'd seen each other. Even though he'd been in a tremendous amount of pain at Brandon's memorial service, suffering as he said good-bye to his lifelong friend and

15

fellow soldier, Cole had tried to console her, watching over her and taking care of her the same way he used to when they were kids.

It warmed her heart to know her brother hadn't died alone in the line of duty and that Cole had been there to care for him until the end. Her gaze panned his face. She took in the dark smudges beneath even darker eyes and couldn't help but wonder, who was taking care of him?

His eyes clouded as they stared blankly at some distant spot behind her shoulder. Hating the unmasked hurt on his face, as well as the awkwardness between them, she touched his arm. The air around them instantly changed. Cole flinched, his entire body tightening as if under assault. Gemma snatched her hand back, his rejection all too familiar. Even though she was all grown up now, a woman who wanted him as much today as she did all those years ago, he'd never see her as anything more than his friend's kid sister.

Just then the puppies broke out into a chorus of howls and Gemma couldn't help but wonder if they were on to something. Maybe the big, bad wolf did exist, and maybe she was staring at him. Perhaps she should heed Victoria's warning and arm herself with silver. There was no doubt that if she wasn't careful the man looming close could shred her heart into a million tiny pieces.

The second Gemma had touched his arm she lit a dangerous fuse inside him. Cole had immediately disengaged, knowing it could only end up backfiring and blowing up in his face. He hated the familiar hurt in her eyes when he recoiled, hated that he'd put it there—again—but he knew nothing good could come from the firestorm inside him, one that had been brewing since their youth. Gemma had tried to hide the pain, the hurt on her face, and she might have succeeded with someone who didn't know her the way he did.

"Gems," he whispered. He clenched his fingers and fought the natural inclination to pull her to him and comfort her like he did when they were younger. But if her body collided with his—one part in particular—she'd know how she affected him. And he couldn't let that happen. He had to stay strong.

Instead of acting on his needs, he took that moment to pan her pretty features, noting the way she'd tied her long, chestnut hair back into a ponytail. His gaze left her face to trail over the supple swell of her breasts as they pressed against her V-neck top. He shifted, uncomfortable as he perused her slim waist and the way her sensuous curves turned a pair of green surgery scrubs into a Victoria's Secret spread. Christ, she was even more beautiful now than she was when they were kids. But no matter what, and no matter how he felt about her, when it came to Gemma, there was a line he wasn't going to cross.

Her assistant came out from the back room. "He's stable and ready to go to ICU." When her words met with silence, her gaze tennis balled between the two, a sure sign that she felt the tension in the room every bit as much as Cole did. "Ah...Danielle will be here shortly. If you guys want to go, we can finish up."

Gemma exhaled slowly and pushed off the counter. "Thanks, Victoria. I'll come in early to check on him."

Cole stiffened. "He has to stay the night?"

"He needs to be monitored for at least twenty-four hours."

"Then I'm staying."

"It's not necessary. My night assistant will be here shortly, and I'm on call twenty-four seven. He's resting soundly and by the looks of you, you should be doing the same."

if I can't expand..." She let her words fall off, not wanting to think of the alternative.

When he went quiet like he was mulling that over, she panned his handsome face. "You know, Cole, you'd be the perfect poster boy for my cause." She somehow knew if he came to the event and shared his stories the benefactors would be tripping over themselves to open their wallets.

They exchanged a long look, unease moving over Cole's face before he asked, "When is this banquet again?"

"Saturday night. Five days from now." She was about to ask if he'd changed his mind when her home phone started ringing. She looked inside her condo, then back at Cole, debating what to do.

Making the choice easy for her, he said, "You should probably answer that." Before he turned from her, he pitched his voice low and said, "Thanks for taking care of Charlie. I'll come by first thing tomorrow morning to get him." When the phone stopped ringing, he took two steps, paused, then shot her a long, lingering look. Her pulse leapt, her body aching to drag him inside to spend the rest of the night fulfilling the fantasies that had been plaguing her since her youth. "It was nice seeing you again, Gems."

Her heart fell into her stomach as she watched him retreat, his leather-clad back holding her attention until he disappeared around the corner. Once he was gone, she stepped inside, locked her door and hurried to the phone, which had started ringing again. She checked the display before answering, even though she already knew who it was, since the call came in at around the exact same time every night.

"Hello, Mother."

"Gemma," she rushed out, her voice frantic. "What took you so long to get the phone? I was sure you were being mugged."

Gemma rubbed her temples with her thumb and index finger. "I'm fine. I had an emergency at the clinic, that's all."

"An emergency?"

"Yes, but everything is fine now."

A pause and then, "I can tell it's not, Gemma." Her mother covered the phone and Gemma listened to the muffled words. When she came back on she said, "I'm coming over there right now."

"No," she hurried out, then worked to put her mother at ease before she showed up on her doorstep. "Everything is fine. It's just..."

"Just what?"

"Cole is back in town."

Silence met her words, and then her mother whispered, "I've heard."

"Oh, I didn't realize you knew." Not wanting her mother to feel hurt that he hadn't been by to visit her yet she hurried to add, "He hasn't been back for long."

"And he went to see you right away?" she said. "Interesting."

"Why is that interesting?" Gemma asked, but quickly decided she didn't want to hear the answer, or talk about Cole anymore. She put a bit of cheer into her tone and redirected the conversation. "I'll see you Saturday night, then? We should have a great turnout."

"Yes, that's why I was calling." There was a hitch in her mother's voice and it had Gemma concerned.

"Is everything okay?"

"Do you remember Mr. and Mrs. Washington? They were at our last charity event."

"Yes, why?"

"Well their son Douglas is back in town. He's a surgeon, you know. Highly respected in his field." Never one to beat around the bush, she added, "He'd make great marriage material, Gemma."

Gemma couldn't care less what Douglas Washington did for a living. Heck, even if he won a Noble Peace Prize or could spin a web and climb the tallest building, she still didn't want to go on a blind date with him, especially if it was set up by her mother. "I told you, I don't need you to find a man for me."

"But, Gemma, you know I don't like you living alone in that downtown condo. The city is dangerous." Gemma's thoughts drifted to Cole and all the times he'd seen to her safety. She got the distinct impression he was eager to step back into the role of bodyguard. She frowned, wondering what it would take for him to see that while she might always have an impetuous side to her, she was an adult now. She made good decisions and was quite capable of taking care of herself.

Her mother's voice pulled her back. "Well, you do need an escort to the banquet, don't you? And it would put my mind at ease to know someone was seeing you home safely."

"I was planning to ask Victoria to come along."

"Oh dear, now how would that look? Last time you showed up without a male escort it had the whole town talking. Imagine if you showed up with a girl."

Gemma could feel a headache brewing. She plunked herself down on her sofa and stared at the vacant condo directly across from hers. "Victoria is my assistant, Mother. And since these events go until the wee hours of the morning I decided to get a room this time and crash at the hotel. So you see, you don't need to worry about me going home to an empty condo in the middle of the night."

"Well you should at least let Douglas escort you there. You know these benefactors are conservative and traditional and are more likely to fund your project if your conduct and morals mesh with theirs."

"In other words, I have to show up on the arms of a respected suitor."

"Exactly," she said and, in a sheepish voice, continued, "Besides, I already told him you'd be delighted to attend the event with him."

"You did what?" Gemma rushed out, shocked that her mother had gone so far as to actually set up a date. In the past she'd been pushy, but never had she spoken on Gemma's behalf before.

"Well you have to go now, dear. The Washingtons are huge benefactors and we wouldn't want to—"

"I know, I know," Gemma said, biting the inside of her mouth to stop from saying what she really thought. "We wouldn't want to offend anyone." Even though her mother was far too forceful for Gemma's liking, she had a kind, caring heart and deep down she meant well. She worried about her only daughter, and wanted what was best for her. After her mother lost a son, in such a tragic way, Gemma couldn't bring herself to say no, or do anything to hurt her. Stallone came up to her. Sensing her distress he plunked himself down between the sofa and coffee table and let loose a whimper.

"It's okay, boy," she whispered. "Everything is fine."

"You'll do it then?"

"Just this once," she conceded. "But please don't set me up again."

"You're a good girl, Gemma."

"I'll let him escort me, but don't expect me to marry him," Gemma warned.

"We'll see, dear," her mother said.

Fearing she was fighting a losing battle and deciding to change the subject she asked, "How's Dad?"

"He's still in Europe at one of his conventions. He'll be home at the end of the month. But enough about your father," she said. "Let's talk about Cole."

Leaving Gemma standing on her doorstep, Cole worked to get her out from under his skin, knowing she was a girl with the right ammunition to rock his world. He hurried back to his motorcycle and walked past her now-closed clinic. As he worried for his dog, it had him considering all the great work Gemma was doing and the importance of her cause.

He wondered how he could help her—outside of attending one of her events. The thoughts of donning a suit, mingling with the rich and famous and talking about his life had him breaking out in a rash. He climbed on his bike, started the ignition and pulled into traffic. A few minutes later he parked beside his old pickup truck at the back of the closed motorcycle shop, and made his way in through the side entrance.

Tired after a long day, all he wanted to do was flop down on his cot and forget about the way Gemma had made him feel tonight. He didn't want to think about how all he wanted to do was drag her into his arms and fuck her long and hard until he got her out of his system once and for all. Although, when it came to Gemma, he feared one taste, one sweet touch of her body, would simply draw him in deeper to a place he had no intention of going.

He opened the shop door to find Jack and two other ex-soldiers playing cards. As they roused each other, the camaraderie making Cole smile, the three shared shots of dark rum and tried to "one up" each other with their stories. Cole looked at the motley crew. They weren't just his friends, mere comrades in the field, they were a brotherhood. Men who had each other's backs in the good times and the bad. Deciding to join them for a round, hoping the alcohol would numb the memories of Gemma and put him fast to sleep so the morning would come quicker, he peeled off his coat and tossed it over a chair.

"You been in battle, buddy?" ex-security specialist Garrett Andersen asked. He gestured toward Cole's bloodstained coat as he unconsciously rubbed the purple scar on his face, a habit he couldn't seem to break, Cole noticed.

Jack arched a brow and slid an empty shot glass across the table as Colby, a former working shepherd, sat at his feet. "Anything we can do?" Jack asked, always ready to stand on the front line with his comrades, whether in the field or in the streets.

"It's Charlie's blood."

The three men instantly sobered, and all eyes focused on him. "What happened to Charlie?" they asked in unison.

He watched the men relax as he explained the whole situation. "He's going to be okay. I'll be picking him up in the morning."

Cole flipped his chair around to straddle it, and his gaze went from Jack, to Garrett, to fellow bomb expert Josh Mansfield. These three guys, these military dog handlers, had all loved and lost animals in the field. He considered the work Charlie had done with him overseas. Then, as he thought about

the four clinked glasses Cole said, "Here's to Operation K9. Let's get to work."

Chapter Three

After a night filled with salacious dreams of Cole, Gemma climbed from her bed. As she made her way to the shower a knock sounded on her door. She grabbed her robe, slipped it on over her nightie and followed a barking Stallone down the hall. Who the heck could be pounding on her door at such an ungodly hour? She peeked out the side window and her pulse leaped when she found the object of last night's fantasies standing on her doorstep.

She unlocked her door and started to inch it open when Stallone stuck his nose into the crack and swung it wide. Gemma faltered backward and Cole jutted his arm out to grab her before she landed with an undignified thud. His hand cupped her elbow as Stallone stood between them, panting and looking to be loved by the hard-assed soldier who had a soft spot for canines.

"Whoa, you okay?" Cole looked like sex incarnate, making any sort of response nearly impossible. She stole a quick glance at the man hovering close, taking pleasure in the way his navy cotton T-shirt stretched over broad shoulders and a hard chest. Her glance dropped to faded jeans that hugged him in all the right places, or all the wrong places, depending on who you were asking. With his hair still damp, the spicy scent of his freshly showered skin wafted before her nose. Her nipples tightened in heated response.

"Cole," she said, locking her knees to keep upright. She looked over his shoulder and tried not to notice the way his work-roughened hands felt on her skin, or the way his touch had fire zinging through her body, one part in particular. Her mind took that moment to consider how those large hands of his would feel on her naked flesh, her bare breasts, deep between her legs. She worked to swallow down the heat searing her blood and asked, "What are you doing here?"

As though suddenly realizing he was still holding her, his hand fell to his side and she instantly missed the warmth of his touch. "I have to get Charlie, and since your place was on my way, I thought I'd drive you to work."

When she noticed the way his gaze dropped to her robe, which had inched open to expose her very short, very skimpy nightgown, she almost tightened the belt but decided against it. The heck with covering up. Let him look. Maybe he'd like what he'd see and finally do something about it. Okay, there was no denying her inner bad girl was at play.

She looked past his shoulders and waved to a neighbor. The elderly lady was watching their exchange with far too much curiosity as she sauntered to the end of her driveway to snatch her morning paper. That's when Gemma realized the state of her hair. She finger-combed it, trying to make herself a little more presentable to the man she wanted in her bed today every bit as much as she did all those years ago.

"I'm not ready, yet. I just woke up."

"I'll wait," he said. She didn't miss the hitch in his voice, or the way he suddenly averted his gaze, staring at the plant in the corner like it was the most interesting thing he'd ever seen. She sighed inwardly. What would it take to get him to open his eyes and look at her like that?

Flustered by the things this man made her feel without even trying, she said, "Come in then, before we give Mrs. Henderson a coronary." She dragged him inside. As he filled her entranceway, his close proximity overwhelmed her senses and weakened her already wobbly knees. "What are you doing up so early anyway?"

"It's move-in day and I want to get Charlie settled before the guys and I start hauling furniture."

She nodded and pointed to her kitchen. "Go press the button on my coffee maker while I shower."

His glance moved back to the slit in her robe and he looked like he was in pain when he asked, "You're going to shower?"

"Of course I am. I just got up." In desperate need of a hot cup of coffee after such a scintillating start to her day, she pointed toward her kitchen to set him into motion. "I won't be long."

Cole shut the door behind himself, and she turned to make her way down the hall. She tore off her clothes and caught sight of her hard nipples in the vanity mirror. Without conscious thought her hands went to them and she let loose a sexually frustrated groan as she brushed her palm over the pebbled buds, tired of taking the edge off herself.

Sure, she'd been with other guys—after all, she was a woman with needs—but most of them cared about their own climax. No man had ever taken the time to get to know her body or figure out what it took to push her over the edge. But Cole... Cole was all about giving and would no doubt take the time to pleasure a woman properly.

As a fine shiver of longing moved through her, the sound of Cole playing with Stallone pulled her thoughts back. She jumped in the shower, turning the water to cool. Twenty minutes later, dressed in a fresh pair of scrubs, with her hair tied back, she padded to the kitchen. When she saw Cole standing there, leaning against the doorjamb with a cup of coffee in his hand, her blood burned hotter than ever and she had to remind herself how to breathe.

He gave her that familiar sexy grin that curled her toes and said, "Milk, no sugar, right?"

She took the cup from him and worked to sound casual. "You remembered."

He tapped his head and turned to the side, making room for her to pass. "I remember everything."

Sexual tension grew in her body as she shimmied past him to grab a muffin. She took a huge bite to hide a cringe, wishing he'd forget the night she'd made a fool of herself in the barn. She glanced at the clock and, looking for a distraction, she said, "Charlie should be awake. We should go. I'm sure he'll be happy to see you."

She discarded the rest of her muffin, took care of Stallone, then ran a toothbrush over her teeth. Once finished she found Cole at the front door waiting for her.

He gave Stallone a scrub behind the ears and asked, "Does he stay here alone all day?"

"Sometimes I take him to work with me, but when I know I have a busy day scheduled I leave him here and call the dog walker."

"I could walk him for you."

As she looked at the man dominating the front entrance her heart beat a little faster. He was harder now, tougher, but neither time nor distance had changed her feelings for him. Since last night's dreams proved she couldn't fight her attraction to him, common sense dictated the less time she spent with him the better. She was already in too deep where he was concerned, and the fact that he gave her plant more attention than her slinky nightie spoke volumes. Perhaps she should start dating some of those bachelors her mother went to great lengths to find. And perhaps she should start giving them a chance instead of comparing everyone to the boy from her youth—a boy who was solid, steadfast and reliable, the toughest guy she knew—because when she did they always came up short.

"Everything okay?" he asked.

"Fine," she answered. "And thanks for your offer, but Stallone loves his walker, and he gets to play with all the other dogs."

She locked up and they made their way outside and walked toward his truck. She climbed inside and her eyes never left him as he circled the truck to jump into the driver's seat. A few minutes later, they were passing rows and rows of houses that all looked similar. A car horn sounded as a sports car sped by them, trying to catch the light before it turned red. When she noticed Cole had gotten awfully quiet she cast him a glance.

She resisted the urge to place a comforting hand on his arm and said, "Charlie's going to be okay. He'll be out playing before you know it."

He smiled and gave a quick nod. "I know. Thanks to you he'll be back in the field with me in no time at all, and once again we'll be working side by side."

"He's going back to work?"

"Damn straight. He loves it and he's good at it." He scrubbed his chin, and she could tell he had something else on his mind.

"What?" she asked.

He tossed her one of his disarming grins, and her insides swirled like an unleashed tornado. "Well..." he began.

She arched a curious brow, and when they stopped for a red light, she asked, "What's on your mind, Cole?"

"Last night the guys and I were thinking about your no-kill shelter and how we can help."

She lifted a hopeful brow. "You guys are going to come to the banquet to speak?"

"No, we were actually thinking more along the lines of taking a few dogs and training them. If we turned them into certified service dogs we could put them into the hands of bomb-hunting handlers here on US soil."

"Cole..." she began, shaking her head. Most of the animals in her shelter were mutts. While she knew you could teach an old dog a new trick, she wasn't sure they could turn them into trained service dogs.

"The dogs will be in good hands, Gems," he rushed out. "These guys take better care of their animals than they do themselves. I can promise you that."

The light turned green and Cole took the corner. "I don't know," she said.

"You of all people know working dogs love what they do and they don't just thrive on it, they live for it. We'd have to work with the dogs individually, to discover if they have the right personality and can follow orders. It'll take a great deal of time, but the guys and I have a whole lot of that on our hands now. It's a win-win situation."

She mulled it over and her stomach clenched when she thought of the alternative. If she didn't make room in her shelter or get the funding she needed, she was going to have to turn animals away. But she still wasn't sure if they could be turned into working service dogs. Then again, she could trust

Cole, and he'd never certify any animal he felt wasn't capable or ready. The fact that he and the others wanted to help touched her deeply.

"Will you at least let me prove I can train them and show you how much they thrive on it?" he asked.

"How?"

"There's an old military base not too far from here. Jack is looking into training them there. I'll prove to you that the guys and I have what it takes and show you how their work can save lives. And once you're satisfied, we can go from there."

When they reached her clinic, he parked and turned to her. Her heart swelled in her chest as she reached for her door handle. When presented with a problem, Cole certainly was a man of action. What he and his comrades wanted to do to help meant the world to her. "Thank you, Cole."

Cole nodded and they climbed from the truck and made their way to her front door. She inserted her key into the lock and he pulled open the door and held it for her. They entered and she gave him a quick tour of the facility as she guided him to the recovery room where Charlie was staying. A wide smile lit Cole's eyes the second he found Charlie waiting for him, his tail wagging madly.

Her heart lodged in her throat as she watched the two reunite. After giving Charlie a thorough examination, she saw them off and turned her attention to her lobby, which had begun to fill up with four-legged patients.

A long time later, tired as the workday came to a close, Gemma walked into her back office. She plunked down in her cushy chair and, after a call to the event planner, she remembered her blind date.

Grimacing, she shook her mouse to wake her computer and typed in the name Douglas Washington. If he was going to be her escort, she at least wanted to know a little bit about the guy her mother wanted to marry her off to. She read his profile, which was about as exciting as a wet crouton, then let loose a long sigh. Honestly, she needed to stop comparing every man she went out with to Cole, otherwise she was going to spend the rest of her life alone. Someday she'd like to get married and have a family of her own, which had her wondering more about Cole. Now that he was back for good, what did he want out of life besides work?

As she thought about Cole, she wondered if he might have changed his mind about attending the charity event. Now that they shared a common goal and he was getting involved in her no-kill shelter, would he want to attend to learn more about her cause?

Benefactors would love to hear stories about bomb-hunting dogs working in the field, and how he and his comrades wanted to train new service dogs and place them in the hands of ex-soldiers. If he took the podium, it would go a long way to help them both. Except Cole was a private guy, one who held his secrets close—compliments of a hard childhood no doubt—and it wouldn't be right for her to ask him to step out of his comfort zone to help her in such a manner. He was already doing enough as it was. And honestly, it wouldn't be fair of her to ask him to dredge up memories from the field. After what he'd been through, it couldn't be easy for him, or any soldier, to rehash those dark days.

A noise at her door had her glancing up from her screen. Ripples of sensual pleasure danced over her skin when she spotted Cole lounging casually against the doorjamb. By God, no man should ever look that good.

Desire turned to worry as she thought about why he'd be here. "Is Charlie okay?"

"He's home resting."

She angled her head. "Why are you here?"

"I thought I'd walk you home."

Knowing it wasn't in her best interest to spend any more time with him than necessary, she said, "I can walk myself."

"It's dark."

"I'm not afraid of the dark."

"You used to be."

"I used to be a lot of things," she countered, remembering how shadows created monsters on her walls when she was young and how Cole would stay with her until she fell fast asleep.

Everything in the way he looked at her, the way he dropped his head and drove his hands deep into his pockets, reminded her of the Cole from her youth. She thought about the boy who'd searched all night for her during a raging thunderstorm when she went riding in the woods and lost her way, a boy who'd held her hair back when she'd snuck out to a party, drank too much and became violently ill. A boy who'd turned into a man and didn't want her the same way she wanted him, which gave credence to her logic to keep her distance from him.

"It's on my way," he said.

She arched a curious brow. "I thought you said you were moving out of Jack's today."

"I did."

The way he averted his gaze instantly gave her pause. She took a moment to focus her thoughts. As understanding dawned in small increments, a slow burn began deep in her belly. She climbed from her chair and braced her hands on her desk.

"You're the one who bought the condo across from mine, aren't you?" she asked, praying she was wrong.

"Yeah," he said. "It's nice and close to work."

Nice and close to work my ass.

Her heart began beating wildly and anger surged through her veins as her brain leaped to the most logical conclusions. "Cole, seriously," she said, shaking her head. "Tell me you didn't buy that place because it's across from mine and you want to keep an eye on me because you still think you need to protect me."

"Gems, it's not like that," he said, but from the way he was shifting his feet she knew it *was* just like that.

"I don't need a bodyguard," she bit out.

"Gems—" he began, swaying like a guilty schoolboy standing before his principal, but when she took in his watchful eyes she cut him off.

"Fine, then," she said. As she moved swiftly across the room her mind raced with outlandish ideas before her inner bad girl settled on the most devious one. "You can play it your way," she added. But that didn't mean she couldn't play by her own rules. If Cole insisted on watching over her, she would damn well give him something to watch. And maybe, just maybe, in the process it would alter his perception of her and he'd finally see she was all woman.

What the hell did she think she was doing?

Night blanketed the city as Cole stood near his living room window, watching Gemma mill about her condo through the crack in her curtains. His condo might be the only one with a direct view into her place, but if someone passed by on the street, they could easily see her barely clad body moving from one room to another.

Dressed in a silky little piece of nothing that had his passion-rattled mind urging him to go over there and fuck some sense back into her, he fisted his hands, drove them into his pockets and rocked back and forth on his heels.

A slow tremor worked its way through his body. His cock, still hard since setting sight on her four days ago, when she'd answered her door in a silky nightgown, was ready to break through its zippered barrier and rise up for a front row seat. Seeing her standing there looking all warm, soft, sexy and sleepy, had him aching to capture her in his arms and carry her straight back to her bed. Once he had her where he wanted her he'd climb between those long legs of hers and bury his mouth in the apex of her thighs—something he'd been dreaming of doing for far too long now. Christ, what he wouldn't have done to spend the rest of that day making her scream for him. And scream she would. He growled, and on the floor near his feet, Charlie, who had healed up quite nicely since his surgery, thumped his tail.

Cole gave a hard shake of his head in a failed effort to clear it. He'd been watching her for three long nights now, going into his fourth, and he was pretty sure the girl next door—one who suddenly seemed more seductive than sweet—was up to her old tricks, teasing and tormenting him to the point of distraction.

"That girl is going to be the death of me," he said to his dog, and Charlie gave a whimper, like he was fully aware of Cole's discomfort.

The light in her living room flicked off. Cole shifted, about to grab a cold beer to help tamp down the heat inside him when her bathroom light came on. Jesus, with her curtains parted he could see her standing in front of her mirror, her hands

47

gripping the hem of her camisole. He swallowed, hard, and tried not to look. He really did. But by God, even though ogling the half-naked beauty across the street was all kind of wrong, there was nothing he could do to tear his gaze away from the woman who'd become the object of his obsession. After all, he was a man, and a man only had so much willpower.

She peeled her top off to expose the most luscious breasts he'd ever set eyes on. As lust settled deep in his groin his cock throbbed, aching for attention. Working to summon a modicum of control as she wiggled, he gripped the windowpane and swallowed down the saliva pooling in his mouth. He couldn't see below her waist, but from the way her breasts were swaying, her long dark curls flaring around her face, he could only guess she was shimmying out of her panties.

Fuck.

She turned her back to the window and reached into her shower to turn it on. If he wasn't mistaken she shot a sassy glance his way before climbing in. Son of a bitch. She really *was* fucking with him.

Cole backed away and headed straight for his fridge. He grabbed a beer, cracked it open and took a long swallow. After draining half the contents in one gulp, he dropped it onto his counter and looked around. If he didn't find something to do with his hands he was either going to take his cock into them or go over there and fuck the hell out of her.

Just then his phone rang and he was thankful for the distraction. He grabbed the receiver.

"Yeah," he said, trying for normal.

"Cole, it's Jack. You busy?"

Cole grunted. Here it was Saturday night and he was home watching the sexy girl next door get ready for her banquet when he should be out prowling. What he needed was a woman to help take his mind off his friend's kid sister and all the ways he'd like to fuck her.

"The guys and I are going to the park to shoot hoops."

"I'm on my way." He hung the phone up and looked at Charlie. "Let's go, boy."

Cole spent the next hour shooting hoops with the guys while the dogs played in the park. But not even the exercise, sweat or camaraderie could help take his mind off Gemma. He continually tripped up and missed even the easiest of shots.

Josh razzed him about being off his game as Cole reached for his towel, deciding he'd had enough. "I'd better get Charlie home," he said, knowing it was a half-truth. Some part of him was anxious to get back to his place, to catch a glimpse of Gemma before she left for her event.

"What time are we on for tomorrow?" Josh asked, taking another shot.

Cole might have spent the last few nights watching over Gemma but his days had been spent at the abandoned base with his comrades. Jack's father had called in a few favors and managed to get approval to use the space. The four guys had already erected a detection wall inside one of the compounds and were now building boxes to take training one step further. Once they had everything in place they'd be able to test the dogs and determine which could be trained.

"Early, I want to be done before the heat of the day hits."

After a round of agreements the guys dispersed. Cole leashed Charlie, tucked his ball under his arm and made the short trek back to his place. When he rounded the corner he spotted a limousine outside Gemma's condo. A man climbed from the back seat. As Cole looked him over, a surge of possessiveness raced through him. Picking up his pace, he closed the distance between them and the second he caught a glimpse of Gemma exiting her condo, his breath left his lungs in a rush.

She was dressed in a form-fitting, sexy black cocktail dress that hugged her curves and showcased a supple body. While his fingers itched to caress her, she accepted the arm of her date. At first she didn't see Cole standing in the shadows, but then Charlie barked, excited to see the woman who'd stitched him up.

She turned, and her hand went to her chest. "Cole," she said, sounding breathless as she peered at him. "I didn't see you there."

"Gems," he returned and switched his attention to her date, taking note of his expensive suit and how everything about him screamed wealth—the kind of guy her mother would want her to marry.

She quickly recovered from the shock of seeing him and said, "This is Douglas Washington. Douglas, this is Cole Sullivan." A pause and then, "Cole and I go way back."

A confused look came over Douglas's face as his glance moved over Cole's sweaty clothes. He greeted Cole with a curt nod before he put his mouth close to Gemma's ear and said, "We're running a bit late, darling." She nodded and he slipped his hand around her back to guide her to the waiting vehicle.

Seconds before she got into the car she said, "If you change your mind, we'll be at Grand Union Ballroom and there'll be an invitation waiting for you at the doors."

Charlie barked and Cole watched her drive off. While he should walk away, considering Douglas Washington was the kind of guy she should be going out with—rich, sophisticated, a guy from the right side of the tracks—he couldn't bring himself to back off. Truthfully, he should be blessing the union, yet there was something about the guy that rubbed him the wrong way. Perhaps it was his arrogance, or perhaps it was simply because he was escorting Gemma to her event.

Either way, he didn't like the guy, and if he wanted to keep the vow he made to her brother, he had no choice but to go to the banquet and watch over her from a distance. He twisted back around, because while he didn't own an expensive suit himself, he knew Jack would. After all, he wasn't known as *Jack of all trades* for nothing, and as the son of a general, he attended many formal events. Ten minutes later, he and Charlie stood outside Jack's door.

He knocked twice, then found Jack staring at him. Colby came over to greet Charlie, and since both dogs were tired after playing in the park, they went to the water bowl before dropping onto Colby's bed next to the television.

"I need a suit," Cole said, giving his friend a glance over, thankful they were the same size.

Jack laughed. "You? In a suit?"

"Do you have one or not?" he bit out, much harsher than he intended. But goddammit, Gemma had completely thrown him off his game and lit a dangerous fuse inside him, one he'd better find a way to extinguish before he did something he could only regret later.

"What's gotten into you? You look like you're ready to go off."

"Nothing," he said, raking his hands through his hair. "Look, I didn't mean to bark, it's just...I think I should go to the benefit tonight."

"You want to go to the benefit?"

"Yeah. If we're going to help Gemma out, I should learn a little more about what she's trying to do over there." While it wasn't a lie, it wasn't the entire truth either. But he wasn't about to tell his friend, a guy who took him in when he had nowhere else to go, that he couldn't stand the idea of Gemma being there with another man. Fuck. There was an unwritten rule amongst his comrades, an honor amongst the brotherhood. They took care of each other's families, they didn't lust after them, and Jack was fully aware Gemma was his late friend's kid sister.

Jack gave him a long, thoughtful look before disappearing into his bedroom. He came back with a suit inside a zipped garment bag. He handed it over and asked, "You sure you know what you're doing, Cole?"

"Yeah," he lied, never more uncertain in his life. "Can I leave Charlie with you? I don't want him alone for any length of time after his surgery."

"You know it," Jack said. "Colby would love the company."

Leaving his dog in good hands, he tossed the fabric bag over his shoulder and hurried back to his condo. He jumped in the shower, then dressed. Close to an hour later, after opting for his truck over his bike, he made his way to the other side of town.

He stepped into the grand entrance and took in the opulence of the upscale hotel. A concierge made his way over to him. "Right this way, sir," he said, guiding him through the lobby to the ballroom at the far end.

A woman sat outside the closed doors and smiled politely as she asked for his invitation.

"Cole Sullivan," he said, trying not to fidget or pull on his starched collar.

"Yes, of course." She sifted through the envelopes on her table until she found the one with his name on it. "But you've missed the speeches," she said and pulled open the door for him.

Cole walked into the dimly lit ballroom and took note of the people milling about. A waiter came by with a glass of champagne. Even though he was a beer drinking kind of guy, he accepted to be polite. Keeping to the shadows, he scanned the room, looking for Gemma. The second he saw her, his entire body tightened with a need that nearly rendered him senseless.

His throat dried as he watched from a distance, taking in the familiarity of her hand gestures as she spoke passionately to a benefactor. As he registered every delicious inch of her, he drew a fueling breath and noted the slow tremor making its way through his body. He worked to bank his desires, but unfortunately, his damn cock refused to cooperate. Watching her for the last few days had played havoc with his libido, and there was no denying she'd gotten under his skin in a way no woman had ever done before. He panned her contours and the sight of her in that sexy cocktail dress evoked a myriad of sinful thoughts, mainly going over there and dragging her to one of the rooms upstairs where he could finally have his way with her.

"Cole," a familiar voice said, and he turned to see Audrey Matthews coming his way, her arms outstretched. Shifting his stance and knowing he'd been caught admiring Gemma, by none other than her mother, he took a swig of champagne to wet his parched throat.

"Audrey, how are you?" He bent to give her a hug. "I've been meaning to call."

Blue eyes that mirrored Gemma's glistened as Audrey looked him over. "Gemma said you were back."

"Yeah, and listen, I meant—"

"Oh, don't be silly, Cole. I know you're busy and you'll come by when you get the chance." She gave him a wink and added, "Besides, you've been in the field a long time and probably had a few oats in need of sowing before you did anything else."

Uncomfortable with the direction of their conversation, especially because he'd been caught lusting after her daughter, Cole tugged on his tie. "I...uh."

She waved a white-gloved hand. "Oh now, no need to be embarrassed." Just then, a woman stepped up to Audrey and spoke quietly to her. As they conversed, Cole studied Audrey, happy to see how well she was doing. The last time he'd seen her she'd had the strain of losing a son all over her face.

When the woman left, she turned back to Cole. "Gemma told me how you, Jack and the others were going to help her cause. You're a good boy, Cole." Her voice dropped, became conspiratorial. "You know, I'm glad you came home when you did. Gemma is living all alone now, and I don't like it one little bit."

"Don't worry, Audrey. Nothing will happen to her as long as I'm around."

She smiled. "That's my Cole. I knew I could count on you." She blew an exaggerated breath. "But I realize you have your own life and until I get her married off and know she has a man in her house to protect her every night, I'll never rest." She blinked up at him. "Promise me you'll stay as close to her as possible until that happens."

"I promise."

As his gaze strayed to Gemma, he watched her back straighten and he instantly got the impression she knew he was here. Her eyes scanned the room and when they locked on his, passion and heat swimming in their stormy ocean blue depths, everything inside him screamed possession.

They exchanged a long look and he swallowed, trying to appear unaffected when her date stepped up to her, his hand going to her lower back.

"They do make a lovely couple, don't you think?" Audrey asked as her gaze locked on Gemma and her date.

"Yeah," he said, biting the inside of his mouth to stop from telling her what he thought. That he'd like to walk over there and punch the guy in the face and tell him to get his fucking hands off Gemma.

Audrey waved to someone on the other side of the room. "Well, I must go, I'm being summoned." Before she left, she said, "I'm staying in the city this month. Do come by for dinner. I'll have all your favorites prepared."

"I will," he promised and dropped a kiss onto her cheek before she stepped away. Less than five minutes after she disappeared into the crowd the music started playing. The waiter made another round and as Cole placed his empty glass on the tray, he worked to pull himself together.

As he watched Gemma's date guide her to the dance floor, tension grew in his body. Everything about the way she moved triggered a craving like he'd never before experienced. With lust overshadowing sensibility, every reason he had for staying away from her suddenly seemed insignificant. Before he even realized what he was doing, he cut through the throngs of people and tapped Douglas Washington on the shoulder.

"I'm cutting in," he said, the bite in his tone letting the other man know he wasn't asking.

Chapter Four

"What do you think you're doing?" Gemma asked as Cole moved in to take Douglas's place.

Strong hands circled her hips. The roughness of his palms felt erotic as he pulled her into a tight embrace, anchoring her body firmly to his. When his warm, familiar scent curled around her, a shiver raced down her spine. She shifted but there was nothing she could do to conceal the telltale hardening of her nipples as they pressed against his even harder chest. Dark eyes met hers unflinchingly. The intensity in his gaze frightened her as much as it excited her.

"Maybe I should be the one asking you that question."

Feeling slightly breathless as their bodies swayed together, not to mention the way his firmness meshed against her softness, she jutted her chin out and asked, "I have no idea what you mean."

"You know full well what I mean," he bit out, appearing more pained with each passing second.

"I'm afraid you'll have to elaborate. The only thing I'm doing is trying to raise funds—"

"That's not all you're raising," he groaned.

"What do you mean?" she asked, feigning innocence.

"Stop leaving your curtains open."

She blinked. "My curtains?" His hand trailed lower on her back, and when his big fingers splayed over her sensitive flesh, the air instantly charged. "I have no idea what you're talking about." As a wave of heated anticipation prowled through her bloodstream, she realized there was nothing impersonal in the way he was touching her.

"And stop parading around in nothing but slinky underwear," he added, clearly not buying her story.

She wet her lips, and gave a casual shrug. "I didn't think it would bother you, considering..."

His nostrils flared and between clenched teeth he said, "You were a kid, Gems."

"Well I'm not a kid anymore now, am I?" she challenged, her pulse leaping with renewed excitement. She had the sneaking suspicion her devious plan had actually worked, and that she'd somehow gotten under Cole's skin.

A strange, strangled noise sounded in his throat as he drew in a ragged breath. "Maybe not." He fingered the silky material on her dress. "But underneath this façade, this life you built for yourself, you're still that same wild child, aren't you?"

Her heart sank. She must have misread him. She steeled herself, waiting for the lecture. "Cole, I..." she began, wanting to make it perfectly clear to him she didn't need his protection.

"I never said I didn't like that side of you, Gems."

Everything in the way his voice softened when he said her name had her realizing she hadn't misinterpreted him at all. A slow lick of flame moved over her flesh and liquid desire settled deep between her thighs. "Well if you must know, I'll probably always have a wild side, but believe me I'm not a child anymore."

His nostrils flared, like he was waging some sort of internal war. He clenched his teeth harder, the muscles along his jaw rippling. Her glance went back to his and when she saw the desire reflecting there, a shudder moved through her body.

Arousal thickened his voice and volatile heat backlit dark eyes full of raw lust when he whispered, "What are we doing?"

Her heart missed a beat. Everything from the tortured way he was looking at her, to the way his body was pressed against hers—one part in particular—spoke volumes. Cole Sullivan, the same guy she'd been lusting after for ten long years, was finally seeing her as something more than his friend's rebellious kid sister. She'd be damned if she wasn't going to do something about it.

Her nipples scraped against his chest and she murmured, "We're doing what we should have done a long time ago."

He frowned and gave a hard shake of his head. He rested his hands on her hips as if he was having second thoughts. "I need to get out of here."

He continued to press against her, his body telling an entirely different story—he wanted her in his bed as much as she wanted to be there.

She wasn't sure about the demons that haunted him or why he'd want to deny himself what his body craved. But now that she had him right where she'd always wanted him, the rebellion from her youth had turned into fierce determination and she wasn't about to let him flee again.

With her body beckoning his touch, she pushed her hips into him. In a voice full of invitation she said, "If you need to go somewhere I have a room upstairs."

He exhaled slowly. "I'm pretty sure that's not going to help me cool off."

"You can take a cold shower." She ran her hands through his hair, went up on her toes and purposely put her mouth to his ear when she added, "Or a hot one."

"Gems," he murmured, his hands circling her hips. Once again sexual tension hung heavy. "We shouldn't be doing this."

"That's where you're wrong. I want you." She ran her hands over his lapels. Even though the tough soldier cleaned up nicely and looked rather dashing in his suit, underneath the clothes he was still that same rough and rugged, fiercely protective guy who hung out at her family's ranch. "I've always wanted you."

"Gemma—"

She molded her body against his, aware of the explosive heat arcing between them. "Why don't you sneak me to my room like you used to do when we were younger, and instead of lecturing me, I think you should strip me naked and spend the rest of the night in my bed, inside me."

She felt a tremble move through him. "Jesus, you can't say something like that to me."

"Why?"

"Because it makes me want to fuck you, that's why."

"Then what's stopping you?"

He frowned, and she could almost hear the wheels turning. "Are you forgetting who you're talking to? I know you better than you know yourself and I know you want the big house with the white picket fence." His fingers bit into her flesh and conflicting emotions passed over his eyes when he added, "I'm not the guy who can give that to you." He opened his mouth like he wanted to say more but stopped himself.

"I'm not asking you for any of that, Cole. All I'm asking for is one night."

His deep growl reverberated through her body. "If I give you what you want, will you close your curtains and stop torturing me?"

"What *I* want?" she challenged, pushing her pelvis against him harder and taking note of the impressive bulge pressing against her midriff. "Are you telling me you don't want it too?"

"Hell yeah, I want it too." He shackled her wrists, removed them from his shoulders and placed them by her sides. His gaze shifted, scanning the room. It occurred to Gemma that the man who was always in control, always so careful and calculated in his every decision, was coming completely unglued—because of her. Damned if that didn't excite her all the more. He leaned into her and put his mouth close to her ear. "You've got five minutes to excuse yourself," he said in whispered words. "I'll be waiting for you near the elevators."

Keeping to the shadows, she watched him exit the room and a shiver moved through her. She'd never seen him so edgy, so intense before. After he left she stood there, barely able to breathe, let alone comprehend what had just happened. Douglas came back to her and his voice interrupted her thoughts.

"Is everything okay, Gemma?"

"I...uh...you're going to have to excuse me, Douglas. Something has come up." Okay, it wasn't entirely true, but it wasn't a lie, either.

"Is there anything I can do?"

"Please tell your folks I enjoyed speaking with them tonight and I appreciate all their support, but I have to run and will catch up with them again later." He nodded and she excused herself. She grabbed her clutch off the table and forced her legs to carry her out the door. She left the ballroom and when she rounded the corner, she found an agitated Cole waiting for her. Her heart leaped and she wondered how she'd ever keep this thing between them casual. Dark eyes locked on hers and her entire body quivered, coming alive with anticipation. She drew a breath to center herself, determined to simply enjoy the physical pleasures between them. Cole had made it perfectly clear he had nothing more to offer.

They moved toward each other and he put his hand on the small of her back to usher her to the elevator. He jabbed the button and then his hand captured hers. As his large, rough palm swallowed hers whole, the sheer strength of his grip and the powerfulness behind it didn't go unnoticed. The second the doors opened he guided her in. She stole a glance at his face and resisted the urge to pinch herself. Was this really happening? Excited by the prospect and eager to finally experience his brand of lovemaking, her blood began pulsing, wet heat flooding her sex.

"Which floor?"

"Nine," she managed to get out, trying not to sound as breathless as she felt.

He pressed the button as her phone started ringing. When she reached for her clutch, Cole stopped her.

"Ignore it," he said, the impatience in his voice filling her with a new kind of excitement.

A few seconds later the elevator stopped and Cole held his hand out. "Give me your key."

She dug into her purse and handed him the keycard. He looked at the room number and glanced up and down the hall to gather his bearings. With determined steps he guided her down the passageway. Once they reached her door, he slid the key into the lock, stepped inside and dragged her in with him.

The sound of the lock clicking into place sent shivers of need racing through her. Catching her by surprise, Cole backed her up against the door. He pressed his hands on either side of her head, caging her in place. Dark, intense eyes stared down at her and she was sure she was going to climax just from the hungry way he was looking at her.

"Cole..." Her heart thumped wildly as she waited for him to say something, to do something. He looked at her mouth. She parted her lips, aching for him to kiss her. When he didn't, she wondered what he was thinking, what was going on inside that head of his.

Before she could ask, he eased away. Silence hung heavy as he put a measure of distance between them. His chest rose and fell erratically, his gaze never leaving hers as he drew in a ragged breath and continued to inch toward the bed until the back of his legs hit the mattress.

At the foot of the bed she noticed a complimentary bottle of champagne chilling in a stainless steel bucket, and a bowl of strawberries next to it.

"It's just sex, right?" he asked, his tight voice drawing her attention back to him. "A onetime thing?"

"Two people scratching an itch," she assured him. "No promises, no regrets."

Heat moved into his eyes and his nostrils flared. "Then come here."

Her nipples tightened painfully as she dropped her purse and took three steps across the room, until she stood before him. Her body ached with the need to feel his hands on her flesh, his lips on her mouth, his cock deep inside of her. He slipped his hands around her waist and her skin came alive. She arched into him, the heat from his hard body fueling the need inside her.

"You look beautiful in this dress." As he fingered the material, his hands scraping her skin, his hot touch sent shockwaves rocketing through her. "But I bet you look even more beautiful out of it." She caught the raw ache of lust in his glance as skilled fingers gripped the zipper at the top back of her dress. He slowly drew it down her spine until he reached the small of her back. "Take if off. Now."

He stepped back as her dress fell off one shoulder. When he grabbed a strawberry and popped it between his teeth, the juice wetting his mouth, her chest heaved and her entire body went up in a burst of flames. Good God, she'd never been so aroused before, so hot for it. Then again, she'd never been with a guy like Cole before.

Excitement coiled through her as she shimmied out of her dress and watched the way his throat worked when she removed her shoes. She unhooked her bra and he licked the strawberry juice from his lips as she released her breasts, freeing them from their confines. With her nipples puckered, eager to feel his hot, wet mouth wrapped around them, she reached for her panties. The slow shake of his head stopped her.

There was a dangerous gleam in his eyes as he grabbed another strawberry and moved closer. He brushed the berry over her lips, then ran it over her throat and between her breasts, going lower and lower until he reached her pelvis. With his other hand, he gripped the thin lace of her panties. His mouth crashed down on hers in a kiss fueled by dark passion as he curled the band through his fingers. A quick tug later, he tore the scrap of material from her hips. His mouth swallowed her gasp of surprise.

He stuffed them into his pocket like they were some sort of souvenir. Perhaps they were a token to remember this night because not only would it be their first, it would also be their last. With his attention back on her, he popped the strawberry into her mouth. He pushed the blankets to the foot of the bed, then gathered her into his arms before he gently tossed her onto the mattress.

came quicker, and she became completely aware of the dangerous storm building inside her.

"Gemma," he growled, his heat reaching out to her and firing her senses in ways that almost frightened her. "You're fucking beautiful." She slid her fingers through his hair. When he lifted his eyes to see her, something potent passed between them, something that instantly brought them to a deeper, more meaningful level of intimacy.

Her body shuddered and she became completely pliable in his arms when he dropped his gaze back to her sex. He ran the soft blade of his tongue over one thigh. His hot breath scorched her skin and the air ripped from her lungs as his mouth came perilously close to the hungry little spot that needed him most.

He brushed his thumb over her quivering sex and his voice sounded broken, fractured when he said, "You're so wet, baby, and I haven't even touched you."

The heat in his eyes licked over her and, as sparks shot through her body, she nearly lost it then and there. "Cole, please," she said, barely able to keep a coherent thought as the man of her dreams took her to places she'd never been before.

He gripped her legs and spread them wide. "Is this what you want, sweetheart?"

Knowing her voice would only fail her, she gave an eager nod. A moment later he buried his face between her thighs, entirely in tune with her needs. He drew a deep breath and filled his lungs with her scent before he gave a long, leisurely lick that nearly had her exploding like a round of C4. That first sweet touch of his tongue to her sex had her hips coming off the bed. She began moving, pressing against him, her body seeking what it craved from the man she'd wanted for so long.

As his tongue seared her and he ignited her blood to near boiling, she continued to writhe until one large hand went to her stomach to anchor her back down, taking complete control of the situation, and her body. Damned if his take-charge attitude didn't excite her.

Good God, there was no denying Cole was as proficient in the bedroom as he was in the field. He clearly knew more about what she wanted than she herself did. As she soaked in his warmth, she handed herself over to him, his to do with as he pleased. Taking control of her pleasures, he continued to feast on her while he pushed a thick finger inside her.

"Cole," she cried out. A small tremor pulled at her core as he stroked her with expertise, running the rough pad of his finger along the bundle of nerves no man had ever before been able to locate.

As emotions and sensations ripped through her, he pressed his mouth hungrily to her swollen clit, while deep inside his deft finger moved with purpose. Her heart hammered, her entire body going up in a burst of flames. She began panting, needing him to end the sweet torment almost as much as she needed him to continue. Heat reverberated through her blood and she licked her dry lips, the world around her blurring as pleasure forked through her.

"Oh, God, Cole." Her sex clenched hard around his finger as he proceeded to push her over the edge. Her body pulsed and vibrated with release and Cole stayed between her legs while she rode out every delicious wave of pleasure.

When her tremors finally subsided, he climbed up her body. Her flesh began tingling again when he took full possession of her mouth. He reached between them and gently stroked her wet slit and she knew he was preparing her for his impressive girth.

She moaned as she tasted herself on his lips. His tongue tangled with hers, pillaging with hungry, demanding flicks, and she suspected he was slipping past the point of no return. He groaned deep and a moment later he inched back. As he pulled away from her his tortured glance moved over her face, his entire body tightening.

"Cole?" Fearing she was about to lose him and praying he wasn't having second thoughts again, her throat constricted and her heart raced like mad. She cupped his face and looked into his dark eyes. "What is it?"

"I want to be inside you, sweetheart."

Relief moved through her. "I want that too."

Trembling hands brushed her hair off her cheeks, then slid gently over her bare shoulders. The small, affectionate gesture elicited a shiver from deep within. Her heart squeezed in her too-tight chest. "I don't suppose you have any condoms."

She briefly closed her eyes in distress. Good God, never in a million years had she thought she'd end up in bed with Cole tonight, otherwise she would have come equipped. She suspected the same for him, because he wasn't a guy who took chances or played with fire without protection. Which meant he hadn't come here tonight with the intention of sleeping with her. Perhaps he'd purposely come without condoms so he wouldn't be tempted.

She opened her eyes and when she caught the intense way he was watching her, a tremble moved through her. "I don't have condoms, but I'm on the pill."

He exhaled slowly and forced a laugh. She could feel his tension building, a firestorm of need that if left unattended, would implode upon itself. "Baby, I haven't been with anyone in a long time, and I always use a condom."

As his voice played down her spine, she ran her thumb over his lips, her body aching for him in dangerous ways. "I'm clean, Cole."

His crooked smile turned her inside out when he said, "I know you are, sweetheart, what I'm trying to tell you is I am too."

"Then what are you waiting for?" she whispered, her body urging her to join with his before she shattered into a million tiny pieces. Trusting him implicitly, she widened her legs in invitation. He fisted her hair and they exchanged a long, intimate look. A maelstrom of sensations bubbled inside her and warned she might not be the kind of girl who could love casually. Especially not with a guy like him.

With single-minded determination, he gripped her shoulders. His eyes never left hers as he positioned his cock at her opening. A second later he plunged deep, pushing all the way up inside her with one hard thrust that stole the air from her lungs. She gave a little whimper as he widened her, filling her in a way she'd never been filled before.

His heart pounded hard against her chest, and the two began moving, both giving and taking as they established a rhythm. The depth of his penetration and the warm familiarity of his scent raised her passion to new, never before known heights.

He drove impossibly deeper and his mouth found hers as he powered into her. Each plunge took her higher and higher until she could feel another spasm pulling at her core. He rammed into her, reaching a fevered pitch. When his breathing grew shallow Gemma got the distinct impression he was trying to slow down but couldn't.

Ribbons of heat moved through her body. She took a fueling breath to concentrate on the pleasure as she gave herself over to the erotic sensations. She gripped his shoulders, moisture sealing their bodies as one as her nails scratched his skin, leaving her mark on him, a reminder of this night. God, everything about Cole felt so good, so right. But some small, coherent part warned that he just wanted her sexually. Nothing more, nothing less.

"Cole," she cried out as he once again pushed her over the precipice. Completely overcome by the heat zinging through her blood, she concentrated on the bliss and dug her nails deeper into his back.

As her whimper filled the room, Cole whispered her name. A second later he let loose a savage growl as her sex clenched around him. She could feel his muscles bunch, his release rapidly approaching as he struggled to hang on. She rode out the pulses rippling through her body and watched the way his dark eyes smoldered as he, in turn, watched her peak. When she squeezed her sex around him, drawing him deeper and deeper into her body, she could feel the blood pulsing hard and heavy in his cock. His nostrils flared and he gripped her shoulders tighter.

"Come for me," she whispered, urging him to let go as her body trembled beneath his.

Control obliterated, breath rushed from his lungs and he pumped feverishly, like something wild had been unleashed inside him. He threw his head back, no longer able to fight off his climax. Ecstasy flitted across his face as he released with hard, hot pulses inside her.

His virility and strength overwhelmed her as he held her tight, so tight it was difficult to catch her breath. He rested his forehead against hers and took heavy, unsteady breaths. With a new closeness between them, he stayed on top of her, warm contentment curling around them. A long while later, he slid beside her and rolled onto his back. She drew a satisfied breath and melted into his side, loving how natural it felt to be with him like this.

He put his arm around her and she shifted impossibly closer, eager to spend the rest of the night snuggled in his arms. She still couldn't believe he was here with her and had given her the best night of her life. It was abundantly clear Cole was unlike any lover she'd ever had and, the truth was, one time would never be enough with him. She wanted him again. Of that she had no doubt. She placed her hand on his chest and played with his dog tags as his heart settled back into a steady rhythm.

She thought more about what he'd said, warning her he wasn't the guy for her and could only give her one night of sex. She wasn't sure what was holding him back, or what he was afraid of, but now that she knew what it took to get him into her bed, she planned to have him there again. Even if it meant unleashing her wild side on him, over and over again.

Chapter Five

What the hell had he done?

Christ, hadn't he said that when it came to Gemma there was a line he wasn't going to cross? But not only had he crossed it, he'd jumped up and down on it, pounded it into the ground and mocked the hell out of it.

As reality inched its way back in, everything inside Cole urged him to climb from her bed and get the hell out of there while he still could. He was about to make a move when Gemma cast him a sideways glance. She rolled into him, pinning him in place as a soft, sexy sound of contentment rumbled in the depths of her throat.

Apprehensions surged inside him and he sucked in a breath, questioning the intelligence in his actions. He'd been greedy. A total selfish prick. But he'd been so goddamn hot for Gemma that common sense had packed a bag and headed south while another part of his body, one that evidently lacked in moral judgment, had ended up calling the shots. Fuck. Hadn't he warned himself that one touch, one sweet taste of her mouth would only draw him in deeper to a place he had no intentions of going?

Except when she pressed her body against his, offering him up a night of casual sex, coherent thought fled. It was all he could do not to bend her over right there on the dance floor and take her fast and hard. *Speaking of fast and hard.* He should have at least tried to slow down. She deserved better than hurried sex from him. But no, he'd been so hot for her for so long now, he'd lost complete control and went at her like a rutting animal. He shook his head, disgusted with himself in so many ways.

Gemma trailed her fingers over his chest. He grabbed her hand to stop her exploration. "I didn't hurt you, did I?"

Passion-imbued eyes blinked up at him and everything inside him tightened when she said, "Hurt isn't the word I'd use."

"I didn't mean to..." he began but closed his mouth when she pressed a soft finger to his lips.

Her blue eyes lit and her plump, well-kissed lips turned up in a smile. "Cole, seriously, it was...*amazing.*" Her glance leisurely traveled the length of his body and lingered over the thin sheet covering his still-hard cock. "In fact," she admitted, those too-honest eyes of hers blinking up at him, "no man has ever brought me to orgasm before."

While a part of him puffed with male pride, there was another part that didn't want to feel anything except physical fulfillment. This thing between them was just supposed to be about sex. He let go of her hand and shifted uncomfortably on the mattress.

She sucked in a breath and he wondered if she too was remembering and savoring every detail of their climax. Gemma was right about one thing, it was amazing. Totally fucking amazing.

"Most times I have to finish the job myself," she confessed.

"You've got to be kidding me?" he croaked out. The thoughts of her masturbating in her bed all alone, running those soft, sensuous hands of hers over her supple body, almost had him rolling on top of her again and going for round two.

"Nope. You're the only guy who has ever really explored my body, really gauged my reactions to your touch. Although I must confess that I haven't been with many guys."

A burn prowled through his blood at the thought of her in bed with another man. *Oh, this is not good.*

"And not only did you bring me there once, you brought me there twice." She gave a lazy, cat-like stretch and when her silky hair fell over his chest, he didn't miss the deep ache still in his core. Here he'd thought one night with her would assuage his need. Except it didn't. In fact, it just added a whole new set of problems.

As he considered the ways she affected him and had so easily gotten under his skin, unease hit like a sucker punch. He cursed under his breath.

He couldn't dispute the fact that having sex with her had created a new intimacy between them, a warmth he'd never felt with anyone, and, the truth was, he had no idea how to deal with those kind of emotions. Fuck, he never should have gone so far with her. The fact that he was the first man to bring her to orgasm—twice—did something to him, something he feared there was no coming back from.

"Why are you telling me this?" he asked between clenched teeth.

She shrugged and her voice was breezy when she said, "I'm just thinking, if it's this good, maybe we should do it again. You know, just two consenting adults having a little fun. Where's the harm in that?"

He pushed his fingers through his hair. As much as he would like to fuck her again, he began, "I don't think—"

Before he could finish her phone rang. She glanced up at him, and he rubbed his temple and said, "You'd better get that."

She pulled an irritated face. "It's probably my mother."

"Or your date," he said, unable to keep the bitterness from his voice as a strong surge of possessiveness cut through him.

"You don't like him?"

Unable to help himself he bit out, "Do you?"

She began marching her fingers over his chest again, then grabbed his dog tags to examine them. "If I liked him, do you think I'd be here, in this bed, with you?"

"Then why did you come here with him?"

She let loose a long sigh. "My mother, of course."

He pushed back onto his pillow and swallowed his guilt. Less than two hours ago he'd promised her mother he'd keep a protective eye on her. He was pretty sure climbing into her bed and putting his mouth and hands all over her wasn't what she had in mind.

"She insisted I needed to attend this function with the right guy on my arm, and apparently, because Douglas is a successful surgeon, he fit the bill." She frowned. "But she's never gone so far as to set me up before."

Cole's gut tightened as her words resonated inside him. He drew back from her both physically and emotionally. Everything inside him warned that he wasn't the kind of guy her mother wanted her parading around town with. Sure, he was good enough to watch over her from a distance, he just wasn't the marrying kind.

When it came right down to it, he was a working-class soldier, a soon-to-be ex-soldier, who couldn't give her the things she was accustomed to, material things the men attending her benefit could provide. Which was why he'd used discretion and walked out of that ballroom without her in his arms. To Gemma, a night of casual sex with an old crush might be fun and games, but she had a reputation to uphold and he didn't want to do anything to dishonor her. Taking her to bed had certainly dishonored her brother's wish, however. Once again, he couldn't help but feel he'd failed Brandon.

Christ, he never should have let lust overrule sensibility and climbed between the sheets with her. Angry with himself, he tossed the blankets off. "I have to go."

Gemma glanced at the clock. "It's one in the morning. Where do you need to rush off to at this time of night?"

"I have to get Charlie. He's with Jack."

He threw his feet over the mattress and her next words, not to mention the soft, cautious way they were delivered, caught him by surprise. "Why did you come tonight?"

A long pause and then, "Because it was important." He neglected to tell her why it was important or how much he hated her being with another man. Christ, he was in trouble where she was concerned, which meant he needed to put as much distance between them as he could.

With renewed purpose Cole climbed from the bed, dressed and slipped out of the hotel room. Gemma didn't say anything as she watched him go and he didn't dare glance back. One look, one tiny glimpse at the well-fucked woman sprawled across the mattress would surely have him changing his mind and crawling right back into bed with her.

Battling his conscience, Cole left the hotel swiftly and jumped in his truck. He took Gemma's panties out of his pocket and stuffed them into his glove compartment. He made his way to Jack's. After evading his friend's shrewd glance and fearing everything about him screamed he'd had the best sex of his life, Cole gathered Charlie and drove home. Once there he stripped off the suit and jumped into a cold shower. In an effort to wash away Gemma's scent, as well as memories of the way they fucked, he grabbed the bar of soap and scrubbed his skin raw.

But the second he hit his bed all his mind wanted to do was think about how sweet she tasted, how warm and wet she was when he pushed deep inside. Goddammit he loved how her body had readily opened to his. He thought about how they had moved together, in sync, like they were meant for each other. He'd never ridden bareback before and everything from the feel of skin on skin, to her softness wrapped around his hardness, to the way he'd splashed his seed high inside her, had generated a new kind of need inside him.

Cole punched his pillow, unable to get comfortable as his cock tented his blankets. He shifted from side to side and spent the rest of the night tossing restlessly, all the while cursing himself for not having more restraint where Gemma was concerned. He was a soldier for Christ's sake, a bomb expert at that, which meant he was disciplined, cautious, a guy who made rational decisions with his head—the one on top of his shoulders. He should have stayed away tonight. He should have left Gemma in Douglas's hands. At least if she fell for the successful surgeon, her mother would be happy. And a married woman would remove any temptation for Cole.

He finally dozed off near dawn and when early morning sunlight lit a column along his floor, Cole climbed from his bed and went to his window. He peered through the curtains and, when he looked into Gemma's empty condo, he couldn't help but wonder when she'd be back. The only way to put her out of his mind was to go for a run, then head to the abandoned base to help the guys design the obstacles. He pushed away from the window and made his way to the bathroom. Another cold shower was definitely in order before he began his day.

Two hours later, he pulled his bike into the base and found the others already there. With the early morning sun beating down on him, Cole parked his motorcycle beside Jack's. He took off his leather jacket and unhooked Charlie from his side cart. Charlie sauntered off to explore as he shut the gate behind him and made his way over to the table saw where Josh was running wood through the blade.

Charlie disappeared from his sight. With the compound surrounded by a chain-link fence, Cole wasn't worried about his dog's safety. Inside the protective barrier, the base still had a few buildings standing and miles and miles of grassland that would be perfect for simulating real training in the field.

"Where should I start?" he asked Josh, who stopped to take a swig of coffee.

"Jack and Garrett are out back pounding boxes together. Why don't you start cutting circular holes in the ones they've assembled already."

Cole made his way around back to where the others had found a spot in the shade. Both Jack and Garrett gestured with a nod and Cole grabbed the jigsaw to get to work. For the next few hours they all worked, talking quietly about nothing and everything. Soon the sun grew higher in the sky and Cole brushed the moisture from his forehead with the back of his hand.

"It will be quitting time soon," Jack said, raking his fingers through his hair. "I need to get back and get the shop opened. Plus, I'm damn near starved to death."

Cole's stomach took that moment to grumble. He set down his jigsaw and balanced his foot on one of the boxes he'd finished cutting. "I can finish up here if you guys want to take off." Losing himself in the monotony of woodworking would help keep his mind off Gemma, but he thought it best to keep that to himself.

Soft footsteps sounded and the hairs on the back of his neck tingled, every nerve in his body alive. He didn't need to turn around to know Gemma was close. Her warm, familiar scent caught on a breeze and when it wafted before his nose, he drew it deep into his lungs. He shifted, uncomfortable as his cock thickened in heated response, eager to push through his zipper and catch a glimpse of the woman who'd rocked his world last night.

"Hey, guys," she greeted, her tone bright and cheery.

Cole turned around and found her gaze scanning the boxes he was cutting.

"Gemma," he greeted in return. "What are you doing here?"

She held her picnic basket out and smiled at both Jack and Garrett. "I thought you guys could use some refreshments. It's pretty hot out here today."

"You didn't have to do that," Cole said as he bent to give an excited Stallone a pat.

"Sure she did," Garrett returned. He gave her one of his infamous grins, the same grin that had a plethora of women around town eagerly shedding their panties for him. Garrett sauntered over to Gemma to snoop in the basket and Cole had the sudden urge to step between them.

Gemma laughed and the sensual sound traveled down his spine. He cleared his throat to prevent himself from moaning out loud. Without conscious thought he ran his hands over the scratch marks on his neck. Realizing how visible they were to anyone who cared to look, he tugged on his T-shirt to conceal the evidence of a well-fucked man.

Gemma watched the action and the two exchanged a private, knowing look before she said to the others, "After what you guys are all doing to help me, it's the least I could do, don't you think?" She pulled out a plastic-wrapped sub and handed it to Jack.

"The least." Jack gave her a wink as he peeled back the wrap and hungrily bit into the fresh roll like a man who'd been eating field rations for too long.

Josh came around the corner. "I smell food."

"There's plenty here." She handed out sandwiches and drinks, then bent to unleash Stallone.

Cole couldn't help but note the way her cotton sundress fell over the soft curve of her ass. As his thoughts careened in a sexual direction, he became fully aware of the way Garrett was staring at her. Cole cleared his throat to draw his friend's attention. He cast a warning glare, letting him know she was off limits.

Garrett shrugged and dug into his sandwich as Cole cracked his soda and took a long pull to wet his parched throat. When Stallone wandered off, he whistled for Charlie, who'd been inside one of the buildings sleeping the morning away. A moment later he came out. When he caught sight of Stallone he rushed over.

As the two canines got acquainted, Gemma turned to Cole. Her sundress flared around her long, silky legs, ones he'd personally climbed between last night and ached to spread wide once again.

"How are things going?" she asked breezily.

He finished off his sub in record time, surprised he could even swallow as memories of last night bombarded him. "Slow but steady," he said. "We should be able to examine the dogs by tomorrow to see which ones will be suited for the exercises."

"Why don't you give me the run down?" she suggested, an air of professionalism about her as she examined the wood boxes. "Tell me how this all works."

Cole unplugged his jigsaw and noted the serious look on her face. There was no sign of the seductive bad girl from last night, which suited him fine. If she wanted to pretend nothing happened, he could play it cool too. In fact, putting the whole thing behind them and acting as if it had never happened was exactly what he wanted to do.

"Sure, come with me."

She gripped her picnic basket and he stole a sideways glance at her as he led her toward one of the old hangars. When she caught him looking she offered him a warm smile that had a tremor racing through him. Okay, if he was so damn happy that she'd had a change of heart and no longer seemed interested in exploring a brief affair, why did he have a lump the size of Texas pushing into his throat? Shit.

Her voice pulled his thoughts back. "When will you be ready to start training your first dog?"

Cole slid the hangar door open. "Hopefully in a couple of days. We'll bring a handful of dogs out here and it won't take us long to figure out which ones have the right personality for the job."

She frowned, and when her teeth worried her lower lip, he took in her contemplative mood.

"What?" he asked.

"I really hope this works out. The benefit didn't go as well as I'd hoped."

"Is there anything else you can do?"

"I spoke to my event planner. She and my mother have been urging me to have an event in Dallas."

"Dallas?"

She nodded. "Mom is originally from Dallas and she still has lots of family, connections and influence there. She'll be able to rally benefactors up for a benefit, and with the right motivational speech, hopefully they'll open their wallets to help. I told my planner to run with it, and see if it was feasible before I committed."

Cole took that moment to think about what Gemma had said to him the other day. While he'd like to be a poster boy for her cause, he preferred to work behind the scenes. Unlike Gemma he hated the spotlight and would rather face a firing squad than a room full of benefactors trying to decide whether he and his working dogs were worthy enough for them to invest in. He wasn't the guy she needed at the podium. Contrary to what she thought, he belonged at the podium about as much as she belonged in the field. Just like her brother had never belonged in the field. He'd only chosen the army after Cole had enlisted.

"I can only hope the next benefit pushes me over the top and I can acquire the funding. Otherwise..."

"Otherwise you have to ask your folks for a handout and that's something you don't want to do, right?"

"If I do I'll never be able to alter their image of me and they'll never see me as professional, one who can take care of herself."

"But you would if you had to, right? To protect the animals?"

Determination passed over her eyes and he could tell she no longer wanted to talk about it when she said, "It's important to me that I do this on my own."

Topic forgotten, they stepped farther into the building. Her eyes lit with curiosity when she noticed a sheet of plywood lining one wall, numerous round holes cut into it.

She put her picnic basket down on one of the old tables and walked up to the wall. She traced her fingers over the wood and poked her hands into the cubbyholes. "What is this for?"

"There are boxes behind the holes. We hide things like smokeless powder, detonation cords and other devices and compounds used in bomb making. We teach the dogs to identify the smells and when they do, they get rewarded."

"With a treat?"

"Something like that." He tapped his leg and called for Charlie. A moment later his loyal Lab came sauntering into the building. Cole grabbed one of the leashes draped over the plywood and snapped it to Charlie's collar. Then he grabbed his trigger and stuck it in his pocket. "Watch," he said.

He guided Charlie along the wall, pointing to each opening in the wood. When he found the box containing the explosive evidence, Charlie barked and sat on the floor, his tail wagging wildly. As Gemma watched on, delight written all over her face, Cole pressed the trigger and a tennis ball went flying across the room. He let go of Charlie's leash, and the dog went running after it.

"That's their treat," Cole explained. "A game of retrieval."

Gemma released the top button on her dress. He was about to say something, but the creamy sight of her cleavage derailed his ability to concentrate. He cursed under his breath and fisted his hands at his sides as his libido roared to life.

Gemma waved her hand in front of her face, and her familiar scent filled the room. "I'm impressed."

He gave a shake of his head to clear it. "Dogs are impressive animals."

She stepped up to him and poked her finger into his chest. "Actually, I think you're impressive." She waved her hand around. "Most men throw money at my cause, but I like that you're a man of action."

There was something very sexual, very suggestive in the way she said action. It had him wondering if he'd misread her. Perhaps she wasn't quite ready to put last night behind her.

When Charlie came rushing back with the ball, Cole pulled it from his mouth and diligently worked to ignore the heat rising in him—a heat that had nothing to do with the hot afternoon sun. He tossed the ball outside. Charlie went after it, never to return.

"It's simple repetition and association," he went on to explain, needing to think about something other than the reactions she was pulling from him. "We just need to do it over and over again until they get it right." As soon as the words left his mouth, and he realized how sexual they sounded, he fought to get them back.

Her laugh was edgy, sensual when she walked over to her picnic basket and said, "Well, you know the old saying, practice makes perfect."

As he thought about what he'd like to practice over and over again with her, despite the fact that they'd gotten it perfect the first time, Jack poked his head in. "Cole," he called out. "I have to head back to the shop and the guys are running to town for a few supplies. Do you need anything?"

"I'm good," he called out, his voice sounding like a strange, strangled whisper as his double-crossing cock tightened with need.

Jack's warrior features softened as he looked at Gemma. "Thanks for lunch, Gemma. I'll see you soon."

"See you, Jack." She waved good-bye and toyed with the next button on her dress.

They listened to Jack's bike as well as Josh's truck rev to life. The sound of gravel crunching beneath their tires echoed in the spacious hangar as the trio disappeared through the gate and down the long dirt road.

Gemma reached into the basket and pulled out a plastic container full of strawberries. She popped one into her mouth and made a sexy noise as she chewed. She held the container out to him. "Would you like a chilled strawberry? It might help combat the heat in this place."

He gave a quick shake of his head and gestured with a nod to the outdoors. He was about to suggest they step outside, but was instantly distracted when she released the second button lining her dress. Cole watched in mute fascination as she trailed her hand over her flesh, her strawberry-soaked fingers dipping terribly close to her cleavage.

His cock grew an inch and he shifted to alleviate the physical discomfort. "What are you doing?" he grunted between clenched teeth.

"Trying to cool off a bit." She gave him an innocent look, but there was a promise of something far more intimate in her tone.

"What we did last night. We agreed it was a one-time thing, right?"

She set down the container and the gleam in her eyes turned wicked. "Wow, I just came to bring you guys some lunch and look at you, wanting to change the terms of our agreement."

He gave a frustrated growl. "Gemma, last night you were the one...wait, you know that's not what..." he began, but his words of protest were lost on a moan when she pressed against him. Unable to fight the natural inclination to touch her as her heat gave him a raging hard-on, his hands circled her waist.

Torn between duty and pleasure, he looked at the woman in his arms. What the fuck was he doing? Christ, he needed to flee as much as he needed to stay. But when she swayed against him, her soft, coaxing body moving against his, and he caught the sexy, needy look on her face, he could feel his resolve melting around the edges.

Her fingers went to the third button and blood pounded through his veins. "I really only know of one way to battle the heat," she murmured, her voice giving way to soft persuasion, "and that's by getting undressed."

Cole briefly closed his eyes in distress, but her sweet, strawberry-scented breath was so hot, so damn enticing on his neck he feared the situation was escalating beyond his power to stop it.

Sexual tension hung heavy and her voice was a low velvet seduction when she asked, "You wouldn't want me to get heat stroke, would you?"

His fingers splayed over her back as her heat bombarded him. While he wanted to walk away, he hadn't finished with her just yet, hadn't even begun to get her out of his system. With need driving his actions, he crushed her against him. A low groan sounded in his throat. Okay, this wasn't what Brandon and Audrey had in mind when they asked him to watch over her. But since he didn't like or trust Douglas, being with Gemma this way was simply keeping her out of the hands of assholes like him, right? So really, in some twisted way he was protecting her.

Jesus Christ, how was that for logical reasoning at its worst?

"The guys," he said, lust and need rising to the surface even though he was playing with fire. "They'll be back."

Undaunted she said, "Then we'd better hurry."

Christ he didn't want to hurry with her. He wanted to lay her out like a buffet and spend hours feasting on her. What he'd give to take his sweet time, to taste every inch of her body and savor every delicious crevice as he brought her to orgasm again and again. She shimmied against him and he sucked in a sharp breath, understanding when it came to her, he might be fighting a losing battle.

He grabbed her by the waist and backed her up, needing to answer the pull in his groin. With little finesse he spun her around and pressed her against the wall. Grabbing both her small hands in one of his, he pinned her arms above her head. His other hand went to her ass. An excited gasp rushed from her lips when he gave her a hard slap.

He whacked her again and when she angled her head to see him, he spotted lust in her eyes. "Cole," she cried out, her voice sounding breathless. A tremor moved through her body as she called out his name, but from the way her cheeks were flushing to the way her hips were swaying, he knew it was from excitement, not fear.

He stroked her ass to soothe the sting left behind. That's when he made a discovery that just about dropped him to his knees. "Jesus, you're not wearing any panties."

"That's because you ripped them off last night, remember?"

His heart raced—okay, galloped—as he pictured her sweet pussy beneath that dress, waiting for his touch, his tongue, his cock. "You only have one pair?"

Her laugh was edgy, breathy as she blew a wispy bang from her forehead. "No, but they were my favorite."

With his mouth close to her ear, he whispered, "I'll replace them." He gripped the hem of her dress and lifted it until her silky legs were exposed. He ran his hand along her inner thigh before driving his knee between her legs to spread them wider.

She moved urgently against his knee, grinding herself on him. Knowing he was hanging on by a frayed leash as it was, he slapped her ass again. "Stop it."

Her loud moan echoed in the building as small beads of moisture broke out on her body. Cole pulled her hair off one shoulder and, as he kissed the crook of her neck, he breathed in her erotic fragrance.

"Is this why you came here today?" He pushed his cock against her ass, the depth of his desire for this woman more frightening than a field of land mines. "Is this what you wanted?"

"Oh, God." She shivered under his invasive touch.

He trailed his hand up her thigh, until he could feel the heat of her sex. He pulled in a breath as desire twisted inside him. "Tell me, Gems. Tell me why you came here," he demanded, needing in the most desperate ways to hear her say it.

"I came here because I wanted to feel you inside me again."

Her sex fluttered against his finger and the lethal softness of her pussy had his body jerking with need. He brushed his finger over her clit, testing her, preparing her.

"So good," she cried out, her hips moving, riding his finger.

Sensual overload fried his brain cells, knowing she was ready for him long before ever stepping foot in this hangar. He ripped open his pants and freed his cock. "Do you need it bad?"

"Real bad," she murmured.

Even though having sex in the hangar was risky, inappropriate, he turned her around and hoisted her onto his hips. "Put your legs around me." When her eyes met his, his heart lurched and his body trembled almost uncontrollably. Jesus, he'd never experienced such a bone-deep want before. The tang of her arousal reached his nostrils and suddenly the need to lose himself in her became so intense it was almost painful.

Muscles bunching, he pinned her against the wall and positioned his cock at her entrance. She wiggled her hips, teasing his crown in an inch. The second her moist heat seared his bulbous head, his lips crashed down on hers. He pitched forward, driving into her, hard, fast and fierce.

She gasped into his mouth and frantic with the need to fuck her again, he said, "Tell me to slow down, sweetheart. Tell me and I will."

Her soft, sexy mewl curled around him. "Harder," she cried out, bucking against him. "Faster."

Sweet Jesus...

Moisture trickled between her breasts and he nearly sobbed with pleasure as he buried himself in her hot, tight sheath. Completely consumed by her and entirely lost in the moment, he began to pound into her—hot, hard strokes that had her screaming out his name.

Through her thin sundress her luscious nipples scraped against his chest. His mouth watered for a taste while some small, coherent part of his brain told him to stop. Told him this was fucking insane. He closed his eyes briefly, but when she wrapped her hands around his neck and said, "I love the way you fill me," there was nothing he could do to pull back.

Her stomach quivered against his as she ran her nails over his flesh. Everything in her intimate touch fueled his desires.

Concentrating on the points of pleasure, he listened to the sound of her throat working as she swallowed. He knew he was being rough, demanding—again—but, seriously, how much more could a guy take?

Primal instincts ruling his actions, he rode her harder. He powered into her until her walls tightened, her muscles clenching hard around him. A cry caught in her throat and a second later warm cream trickled down his cock. His dick throbbed, his balls tightened in response.

Heat surged through his veins and he inched back to look at her. The desire reflecting in her eyes as they met his instantly had him longing for things that weren't meant to be his.

"Oh, God. You make it so good." Her breath came in shallow bursts as her hips swayed. "No one has ever made me feel like this before."

"Look at me," he demanded.

Her lust-saturated eyes went back to his as she rode out her climax and there was no denying he loved watching her peak, loved knowing he could do this to her.

As her tremors subsided, she buried her face in his neck, her long lashes fluttering against his skin as their bodies rocked together. He sank every last inch into her and she pressed her lips to his shoulders. Her mouth was hot against his skin and it was all he could do to draw in air. She scraped her teeth over him and his body convulsed almost violently.

With basic elemental need taking over, he slammed once, twice, before angling his stance for deeper thrusts. He drove into her with such a force he feared they were going to break the wall. On the next thrust, he threw his head back and came on a growl, splashing his seed inside her. They stayed like that for a long time, his cock so snug inside her he never wanted to pull out. He finally stopped pulsing and the world around him began to right itself. Although, after a second round of sex with Gemma, he feared nothing would ever be right again.

She touched his cheek. "Hey," she murmured. Warm contentment crossed her face and he felt a possessive tug on his emotions.

"Hey yourself." He looked at the cold cement wall behind her and could hardly believe he'd fucked her here, in a rundown old army hangar. "Are you okay?"

"Better than okay."

"I shouldn't be taking you like this, Gems." Not like this. Not with her.

"Maybe I like it like this."

He opened his mouth and was about to tell her that next time it'd be different, that he'd go slower, but he slammed it shut again. There wasn't going to be a third time. Hell, there wasn't even supposed to be a second time, but for some goddamn reason he couldn't seem to resist her.

His body tensed and, by small degrees, he pulled out of her. This was a very dangerous game they were playing. Her feet slid to the floor, her dress falling back over her legs. He looked around and when he saw her picnic basket he said, "We need to get you cleaned up." He opened it, and pulled out some napkins. Her eyes never left his as he put his hand back between her legs to wipe her clean. He cleaned her thoroughly, then stuffed the napkin into his pocket to dispose of later.

She palmed his face and dropped a soft kiss onto his mouth. "Do you have any idea how sweet you are?"

He forced a laugh. "You must be mistaking me for someone else." Hell, he wasn't sweet. He was a selfish prick who was failing everyone around him. Cole fisted his hands. When had he become so fucking weak?

91

The sound of Josh's truck pulling back into the yard kicked his thoughts back to the present. He zipped up his pants and gave Gemma a once-over to make sure she looked presentable. The last thing he wanted was for his comrades to know what he'd been doing with her in here.

She tucked a long dark lock of hair behind her ear and moistened her lips. "I'd better go."

"Yeah," he said, for lack of anything else as he raked shaky fingers through his damp hair.

"I'll see you later, then."

Cole stood there, barely able to think, let alone breathe, as she exited the hangar, a little extra sway to her pantiless ass. He gave a hard shake of his head. How the hell was he going to keep his distance *and* keep his cock in his pants? It was seriously time to put her out of his mind.

Before she left she popped another strawberry into her mouth and tossed him a devious smile. "Or should I say, *you'll* be seeing *me*."

Cole fisted his hair, his pulse pounding hard in the base of his throat. "Jesus, Gemma, what the hell am I going to do with you?"

Gemma turned back around to face him and said, "I'm looking forward to finding out."

Chapter Six

The bell over the clinic door jingled and pulled Gemma's attention. Sitting at the front counter with her assistant, she glanced up from the computer monitor. Her heart raced a little faster when she spotted Cole and his comrades walking into her reception area. Talk about sex in a uniform. Perched on the stool beside her, Victoria gave her a little nudge beneath the countertop, a squeak catching in her throat.

Gemma knew exactly how her assistant felt. The sight of those four sexy soldiers, all dressed in their army fatigues nonetheless, was like a serious case of testosterone overload.

Tamping down the sudden rush of heat zinging through her blood, Gemma pushed away from the monitor. She put on her best professional face and introduced Victoria to the men who were here to help with her cause.

After a round of greetings, Gemma waved her hand toward the door leading to the back shelter. "If you will all follow me, I'll show you where the animals are kept. Each cage has a small doggy door that leads to a fenced-in grassy area out back, so perhaps it might be best if you introduced yourselves to the animals in their familiar surroundings before taking them to the base for training."

Cole stepped up behind her. There was nothing she could do to ignore the tremor it elicited from deep within as his warmth and sheer virility reached out to her. His body was so close to hers sparks arced between them, so volatile and explosive she wondered if the others in the room could feel the energy.

She opened the door to the shelter and was greeted with a round of howls. She stepped up to her oldest and most gracious guest. "Hey, Nana, what's all that barking about?" She bent as the men disbursed to examine the canines. Their military issue boots echoed on the cement floor as they walked down the long corridor.

Cole moved in beside her and he stuck his hand into Nana's cage to give the old girl a pat. As Gemma watched his big palm brush over her black, molted fur, a hand with so much strength and power yet touched with such gentle care, her heart turned over in her chest. She cleared her throat and glanced up at Cole.

"What do you think of Nana here?"

He frowned and stepped closer. The way he crowded her, like he needed to touch her every bit as much as she needed his touch, filled her with a new kind of warmth. "Nana's kind of old, Gems." At the mention of her name, Nana wagged her ratty old tail, excited to finally be noticed and played with. "Has she been here long?"

"Yeah, sadly enough. I would love to take her home but I don't have the room."

Anger moved into Cole's eyes. "How does someone abandon an old girl like her?"

"I don't know. Some people shouldn't be allowed to have pets."

"Or kids," he added with a disgruntled laugh.

"Or kids," she agreed in a soft tone, knowing he was thinking back to his own childhood. For a brief moment she wondered more about Cole's demons. Would he shy away from family and kids because his own upbringing had been less than loving? Or did the affection her brother and parents bestowed upon him show him caring families do exist?

Behind them Josh bent down to see a litter of collie and terrier mix puppies. They all started yelping in unison, each vying for the soldier's attention. Gemma threw her hands up in the air. "Everyone wants a puppy."

"Speaking of puppies," Victoria said, coming into the back room. "Your two o'clock appointment is here."

Gemma spotted a young girl accompanied by her mother and father following Victoria into the back room. She inched away from Cole and smoothed back her hair. "Go ahead and look around." She handed Cole her master key. "Take them to the dog run and I'll check in with you later." She gestured with a nod to the young family of three and mentally went over their adoption file to remember their names before explaining to the men, "Larissa is here to adopt a new pet."

Cole touched her arm to draw her back to him. He put his mouth close to her ear, his words for her and her only. "I'll catch up with you later. There are some things we need to sort out."

While his comrades examined the canines through their cages, Cole turned away from her and started to walk the length of the shelter. Gemma worked to get her focus on the task at hand and off the sexy soldier she wanted again in the worst way. She dropped down on one knee to face the young girl who couldn't be more than four years old.

"How are you, Larissa?" she asked.

"I want a puppy." Her big brown eyes lit with excitement as she clapped her chubby hands together.

"Well you certainly came to the right place," Gemma said, laughing. She reached for the girl's hand. As Larissa slipped her fingers into Gemma's palm, her heart hitched, just a little. Seeing her sweet face had Gemma thinking how much she wanted to have a family of her own someday. Cole was right. She did want the house with a white picket fence. Maybe he did know her better than she knew herself. But it did have her wondering more about Cole, his demons and all the secrets he held close.

"Personally I'd like one that's already house trained," Larissa's mom said, bringing Gemma's thoughts back as the woman crinkled her nose in distaste.

"No, a puppy." Larissa's blonde curls flared around her head as she shook it.

Larissa's father grinned and threw his hands up in the air in defeat. "I guess it's a puppy, then," he said, but from the warm, loving look in his eyes, she could tell he was happy about the choice and that he'd do anything to please his sweet daughter.

She guided Larissa over to the pen full of puppies and the girl squealed in delight. Gemma pulled open the door and when the child rushed in, the hairs on Gemma's arms lifted. As an uneasy feeling moved through her, she glanced over her shoulder. She caught Cole watching the young family, a barrage of haunted memories brewing in the depths of his dark eyes. In that instant everything inside her went out to him and her heart squeezed painfully.

Jack stepped up to Cole and he turned away. She swallowed down the rush of emotions and understood that no matter how horrible his childhood had been, it had somehow shaped him into the incredible man he'd become today. But it didn't change the fact that somewhere deep inside him, that little lost boy still existed. A boy who needed a family every bit as much today as he did all those years ago.

When Cole and the others disappeared out back with a handful of dogs, Gemma turned her attention to Larissa. She spent the next hour helping her find the right dog for her family. Once done and the papers were signed, she saw them off and made her way to the back shelter to check on progress.

She found Victoria standing in the doorway, watching the men toss tennis balls to the animals in the grassy pen out back.

"How's it going out there?" Gemma asked.

Victoria released a long sigh. "I think I'm in love."

Gemma laughed. "Which one?"

"All of them." Victoria cast her a curious glance, her green eyes dreamy. "What about you?"

"What about me?"

"Oh come on, Gemma. I don't know who you think you're fooling. The heat in Cole's eyes when he looked at you nearly set off the fire alarms."

"We're friends. We go way back," she said, not wanting to share a single detail with anyone. She wanted to keep the memories deep inside her, where she could savor them in their entirety.

Victoria huffed. "Yeah, well I want a friend like that."

The bell over the door jangled once again. "That's my three o'clock," Gemma said. "Will you see to it that the guys get what they need?"

Victoria arched a playful brow. "Oh yeah. I'd be happy to give them anything they need."

Grinning, Gemma left the back shelter and went off to finish her afternoon appointments. By the time she was done, the guys had left and she was sorry she hadn't gotten a chance to speak with them. She was curious to see if they'd had any success.

Knowing it was quitting time and Victoria and her other staff had already left, Gemma made her way to the front lobby. Danielle was just arriving as she reached for her purse.

"You're a bit early," Gemma said to her night assistant.

Danielle frowned. "There's a storm moving in and I wanted to get here before it hit." She glanced out the front window. Worry darkened her brown eyes when she turned back to Gemma. "They're calling for thunder and lightning."

Gemma nibbled her lower lip, and considered the animals. "Maybe I should stay."

"I got this, Gemma. You've been here all day and need to go home to rest."

"Okay, but if you need me you'll call, right?"

"I will."

Gemma stepped outside and listened to the lock click in place as Danielle locked up behind her. Once she reached the sidewalk, she glanced at the overcast sky. Heavy clouds threatened, and she hugged herself. There was no denying she hated thunderstorms as much as the animals in her shelter did. She hurried home, and when she reached her stoop, she spotted a package on her front doorstep. She glanced around. Who could have left her a parcel?

As cool mist fell over her body, she gathered the package and rushed inside. Stallone greeted her at the door. Before she could tear into the paper, she had to take him for a walk. She hurried back out the door, but when the rain started picking up Stallone looked up at her, his big brown eyes conveying without words how much he hated storms. She rushed him to the park where he could do his business in a hurry. Once finished, they raced back home before the skies opened up.

Inside, she fed and watered him, then turned her attention to the package. She flipped it over in her hands, but there was no return address or any markings to indicate where it had come from. Having no idea who would have left something on her doorstep, she tore into the brown paper and couldn't help but laugh at what she found inside. Big. Oversized. Granny. Panties. So this was what Cole had in mind when he said he'd replace the ones he'd ripped.

She held one pair up in her hand to examine them, then padded to her window. She inched open her curtains and spotted Cole watching her. From her distance, not to mention the fact that he was standing in the shadows, she couldn't make out his features. She did, however, suspect he was standing there with that familiar grin on his face, one that said he'd won the battle. Okay, she'd give him this one, but she still had every intention of winning the war and getting him back into her bed again. She laughed again, loving that youthful, playful side she hadn't seen in so long.

She twirled the panties around her finger as a mischievous idea bounced around inside her brain. Deciding she would wear his gift and little else, she tore off her pants and thong and stepped into the huge pair of panties, drawing them up until they nearly doubled as a bra.

Turning from the window and making the decision to carry on as she always would, she caught her reflection in the living room mirror and cringed. Now how was that for attractive? But she'd play it his way. For now. She went to her kitchen to prepare dinner, answered the phone when her mother called and went about her night as usual. Every now and then she'd glance across the street to give Cole a knowing, seductive smile.

By the time her bedtime rolled around, the rain was coming down harder, pelting against her window in a steady pattern. Stallone rushed down the hall to her bedroom with her. She discarded the granny panties and pulled on a cotton nightgown, then climbed between the sheets. Drawing them to her chin, she listened to Stallone whine as he dropped down beside her bed.

"It's okay, boy." She soothed her hand over Stallone's head, even though her insides were wound tighter than the pups during a full moon.

She lay in her bed for a long time, the heavy rain sending her memories back in time, specifically to the overcast afternoon when she was fifteen. She'd taken her horse, Mandy, out for a long run and had somehow gotten off the beaten path. Soon day had bled into night and a storm moved in overhead. When thunder rumbled, it spooked her horse. Catching Gemma off guard, a frightened Mandy had gone up on her hind legs, knocking Gemma to the ground. Gemma had found shelter beneath a tree, but not too far from where she'd been sitting, lightning struck a branch and the forest flared to life around her. Panicked, she'd found herself surrounded by flames, and it was then that Cole had found her. Alone. Wet. Horribly frightened. He'd packaged her in his arms, brought her to safety and refused to leave her side until she'd fallen asleep. If it wasn't for him, she hated to think what might have happened.

Gemma tossed and turned until exhaustion finally took over and she drifted off. She had no idea what time it was or how long she'd been asleep when a rumbling sky and a brilliant flash of light outside her window pulled her awake with a start. Heart pounding, she sat up in her bed. Stallone started howling.

"It's okay, boy." She flicked on her lamp and sank down onto the floor beside him. Rubbing his ears, she tried to pacify him as best as she could. She pulled a blanket down with her and covered them both as another flash lit the sky. She counted the seconds in between flash and roar. Her heart raced faster when she discovered the storm was directly overhead.

She thought of the animals down at the shelter and how agitated they'd be. Nana would need her. She reached for her robe and her hand stilled when a loud knock sounded on her door.

Cole.

Her heart pounded wildly as she climbed to her feet, pulled on her robe and opened her bedroom door. Despite the storm, her protector Stallone barked and rushed down the hall in front of her. Gemma followed, hugging herself as lightning lit up her condo with noonday brilliance. She peeked out the side window and when she found a soaking wet Cole standing on her doorsteps, she unlatched her bolt, relief racing through her.

"Cole," she rushed out, her words swallowed by the thunder overhead. Not knowing whether to laugh or cry she grabbed his wet shirt and hauled him inside. Charlie came rushing in after him.

Instantly stepping into the role he performed so well, Cole put his arms around her and held her tight. "Are you okay?"

The second she felt his strong embrace, she realized how *not* okay she was.

"I saw your light."

"Cole," she murmured. "I just don't like…"

"It's okay, Gemma. I'm here." He stroked her hair and pressed his lips to her forehead. His kiss, far more emotional than physical, took her by surprise. "You're safe. Nothing is going to happen. I promise."

With her insides reeling, she sagged against him. He held her tight, and when she wrapped her arms around his waist, it occurred to her how right it felt to be held by him. Cole was the only man who ever made her feel warm and safe. She breathed in his familiar scent and let it calm the storm inside her.

"Is Charlie okay?" she asked.

"He's fine," he whispered into her hair. "He's a bomb expert and is used to loud noises. He might even be able to help calm Stallone." As if on cue, Stallone whined and Charlie nudged him with his muzzle.

She lifted her chin to meet his eyes. When she saw the tender concern in his gaze as it met hers, her heart turned over in her chest. God, she was in so much trouble. "We need to get you out of these wet clothes."

"I'm okay." He inched back and scanned her face, assessing her. "Coffee?" he asked, a tactic to distract her from the storm and give her something to do with her hands, she assumed.

Just then, her house shook and the power blinked off. She looked up at him and he pulled her back against him. As her body pressed against his, he tightened his grip and he rested his chin on the top of her head.

"I was actually thinking I should head to the shelter. Most of the animals are afraid of storms and it might help if I'm there."

"I'm coming with you."

"You don't have to do that."

"I didn't say I had to." He eased back and looked at her. "You know, Gemma, it's okay to ask for help sometimes. It's also okay to accept it when it's offered. It doesn't mean people won't think you're capable of taking care of yourself or that you're not all grown up. Everyone needs someone sometimes."

"I'm glad you're here, Cole." She was about to ask if he ever needed anyone but when he captured her hand in his her words fell off—once again the protective soldier was about to give instead of take.

"Come on," he said and led her down the hallway and into her bedroom. He ushered her to her bed and sat her down. "Where will I find your clothes?"

"I can get them."

The house shook again and there was nothing she could do to stifle the sound crawling out of her throat.

"Stay put, Gems. I can get them."

Conceding, she said, "There's a pair of scrubs in my top drawer."

He walked to her dresser and pulled it open. As she watched him move with confidence, she had to admit, even though she was all grown up and trying to prove herself, she kind of liked it when he took care of her. He handed her a pair of scrubs and when eyes full of worry met hers, her insides quivered. As emotions rolled through her, her stomach clenched. She suddenly felt like she was freefalling without a net. God, this was not good, not good at all. Cole said he could only offer her one night of sex. Her mind flashed back to Victoria's silver charm bracelets, and she silently cursed herself for not armoring herself better.

Then again one night of sex had turned into two. Would it be possible for sex to turn into something more? Did she dare hope?

His hand stilled when he spotted the package he'd sent her on top of her bureau. He grabbed a pair of panties and arched a playful brow.

"No," she said, answering his unasked question. "I am not wearing them. My panties are in that cabinet." She pointed to her lingerie chest.

"Yeah, well, these didn't work anyway." He grunted something under his breath as he tossed the granny panties back onto her bureau.

"Didn't work?"

"I saw you parading around in them and it still made me want to come over here." His jaw clenched. "I swear to you, Gems, if you don't cut it out, I'm going to sew your curtains together."

The tortured look on his face eased the tension inside her. She was about to ask why he hadn't come over but her words dissolved when the lights flicked on then off again.

Cole frowned. "We'd better hurry." He pulled out a bra and matching pair of panties from her chest and brought them to her.

He turned his back to her, giving her privacy.

She stood and slipped off her robe. "What, you're not going to watch?"

His body tightened. "No, I'm not going to watch."

"And here I thought you liked watching," she murmured under her breath.

"Gems," he said, his voice sounding tortured. "If I turn around there is no way we'll get to the clinic."

"Oh," she said, a little breathless. While she liked the idea of that, the dogs needed her so she quickly pulled on her scrubs.

Once she was dressed, Cole followed her down the hall. When they reached the door she grabbed her raincoat.

"Wait here. I'll get the truck." He looked at Charlie. "Take care of these two until I get back." Charlie barked, like he knew exactly what Cole was saying.

Gemma stood inside her door, both Stallone and Charlie beside her. Rain pelted hard, blurring the streets and obscuring her vision. When Cole's headlights flashed in her driveway, the dogs bolted. She locked up and followed them down the stairs. Cole had both dogs secured in the truck when she reached him. She jumped in next to them and he shut her door and ran around to the driver's side.

Water dripped down his face and his hair was plastered to his forehead. He used the back of his hand to brush it away.

She touched his forehead to swipe at a fat drop. "You need a raincoat."

"A raincoat was the last thing on my mind. When the storm hit overhead, all I could think about was you. I know you don't like thunder and lightning." He cast her a quick glance before turning his eyes back to the road. "I was there that night, remember?"

"I remember," she said quietly. Her heart fluttered as she listened to the rush of the windshield wipers. "Always my protector," she murmured and he gave her an apologetic look. And why wouldn't he look sorry? Hadn't she blatantly told him she didn't need him looking out for her? Except it was ingrained into his nature, she reminded herself, and once again she couldn't deny there was a part of her that secretly liked that about him.

Less than five minutes later, Cole pulled his truck up in front of her work. She opened the door and the dogs hopped out with her. As he parked, she grabbed her key and opened her clinic door. She tried the lights, but the power was off. Hugging herself, she stood inside waiting for him. The dogs were howling in the back. Worry moved through her, knowing Danielle had her hands full. When she spotted Cole rushing down the sidewalk, she pushed the door open for him.

Thunder and lightning hit again and Stallone yelped. "Let's put these two in my office. There are no windows and it should be quieter." Cole agreed and after they secured the two dogs away from the windows, they made their way to the back shelter.

Gemma opened the door and as she rushed to Nana, she looked for Danielle, who was nowhere to be found. Panic moved into her stomach and she reached inside Nana's cage to brush a soothing hand over her muzzle.

"What is it?" Cole asked, from behind her.

"I don't know where Danielle is."

A gust of wind caught the back door leading to the grassy area and it flew open. Gemma jumped when it smashed against the wall. Cole caught hold of her. "She must be out back."

They hurried to the door. In the dark Gemma caught a glimpse of Danielle trying to rustle the howling dogs back into their cages.

"Dammit," Gemma said. "We didn't lock the doggy doors. The animals are spooked and trying to run away."

"Danielle," she called out, her voice catching in the wind as it whipped her hair around her face.

Danielle spun around. Relief moved over her mud-coated face when she saw Gemma and Cole there to help. She held up one of the howling pooches. "They got out," she yelled over the wind.

"We need to rustle them up and lock them in," she alerted Cole. Gemma moved farther into the grassy area, the heavy rain turning the ground to mud beneath her. Her feet sank in and she slipped, going down on her hands and knees, mud splattering her face and hair. She sputtered and cursed herself for not putting on her rain boots as Cole helped her to her feet.

"You okay?" Cole brushed mud from her cheeks as the heavy downpour matted his shirt to his skin.

"Yeah, let's split up."

In the dark, Gemma followed the sounds of howling dogs and gathered up a few muddy animals. After securing them inside and locking their doggy doors, she trekked back out into the rain. Close to a half an hour later, with each dog finally secure in its kennel, they made their way inside to the shelter area.

Standing in the long corridor, lightning struck. Gemma tried to slow her heart rate as she counted the seconds until the rumble hit. "Looks like it's passing."

"Thank God," Danielle said.

Gemma made her way to Nana's cage to kneel down beside it. "It's okay, girl," she whispered to the trembling dog.

Nana gave a yelp and her tail wagged harder when Cole came over. Everything from his dirty clothes to the streaks of mud on his face and the way he came to her rescue tonight had a lump pushing into Gemma's throat.

"I think she likes you," Gemma said, then scowled playfully. "What's with these dogs and their bad judge of character?"

Cole gave her a cocky grin, and spoke soothing words to Nana as Danielle tried to wring mud out of her long ponytail.

Gemma stood and she cringed when her hands went to her own soaking wet hair. "I don't think I'll ever be able to get the mud out."

"Thanks for coming to help." Danielle frowned. "I tried to call but the phones were down, and I couldn't seem to get service on my cell." She shook her head. "I still can't believe I forgot to double check the doggy doors."

"Don't beat yourself up. It's happened to me before too." Gemma looked at her young assistant, who'd been through a lot tonight. "Why don't you head home, Danielle. I can take over from here."

"No, you don't have to—"

"I insist." She put her hands on her assistant's shoulders and turned her toward the front reception area. "I slept earlier and I can crash on the sofa in the back lounge if I get tired. The storm is almost over and the dogs are already starting to settle. You need to get home and get cleaned up."

Danielle shot a glance over her shoulder. "But you need to get cleaned up too."

Gemma slipped off her muddy raincoat and set it on a hook to dry. She toed off her shoes and said, "I keep fresh scrubs in my office and I can shower in the lounge."

"If you're sure."

"I'm sure."

Conceding, Danielle made her way to the front and Gemma turned to Cole. With heavy-lidded eyes, she gave him a tired smile. "Thanks for everything tonight." She paused, looked over his mud-coated clothes and added, "I think you owe me a dry cleaning bill." She took two steps toward the front clinic. "Come on, I'll walk you out." The hand on her shoulder stopped her. She spun back around.

Something warm moved over Cole's eyes. "Did you think I was leaving?"

"I thought—"

The power flicked back on as his mouth closed over hers and his kiss was so achingly gentle, her entire body weakened. After a long moment he broke the contact. "Come on."

"Where?" she asked, wondering how she managed to push that one word past the lump in her throat.

"The storm's not over yet, and I'm not about to leave you." He captured her hand and led her from the back shelter to the front door. He set the deadbolt, pulled her closer and guided her down the long hallway, leading to her employee lounge.

Once there he directed her to the shower area at the back. He pushed open the door, ushered her inside, then locked it behind them.

"Cole?" she asked, her stomach fluttering as his presence swallowed up the small room.

"Shhh," was all he said as he reached into the shower to turn on the hot spray. He adjusted the nozzle and steam filled the space as he lowered the lid on the commode and crooked his finger. "Come here."

Gemma stepped up to him. He widened his legs, gripped her hips and, in a move that was all male, pulled her in between his thighs. A warm, intimate silence fell over them as his hands went to the hem of her shirt. Acting like it was the most natural thing in the world, he began to undress her. He peeled off her mud-soaked top, reached around to unhook her bra and tossed the wet garments to the floor. Next, his hands went to her drawstring. Deft fingers loosened the knot and when he widened the waist and let go, her scrubs fell to her ankles. Touching her in such a familiar way, he gripped her panties and hauled them down, tapping one leg for her to lift it.

Once her clothes were removed she stood there, trying to remember how to breathe as he, in turn, stood and pulled off his wet shirt and jeans. Warm steam filled the room, and everything in what he was doing seduced her senses in the most profound of ways. His expression was tender, the look in his eyes attentive and thoughtful when he put his hand on the small of her back to guide her into the hot, needle-like spray.

They both stepped into the small, tiled area and Cole closed the floor to ceiling glass door behind them. The hot water acted like a soothing balm to her cold skin. She let it flow over her naked body and soothe her ragged nerve endings.

Cole moved under the spray with her, turning her around so her back was pressed to his chest. As she pushed against him and his hardness meshed against her softness, a need so frightening it had her shuddering warned she might be in way over her head where he was concerned.

He tilted her chin back to soak her hair before squeezing a generous amount of strawberry-scented shampoo into his palms. He lathered her hair, his touch shockingly intimate as he ran his fingers through the stands to clean the mud. The sheer intimacy in the way he was taking care of her nearly stopped her heart.

He reached for the soap and lathered her quivering body with his hands. His palms slicked over her flesh. His touch warming her from the inside out as he washed the night from her flesh. Starting with her throat, he ran his soapy palms over her shoulders, her breasts and her stomach. Then he turned her to face him while he reached around her to scrub her back.

Her breasts pressed against his chest and when she tipped her head to look him in the eyes she became spellbound by what she met there. Possessed by his stare as it touched something deep inside her, her pulse leaped in her throat. Silence ensued as they looked at one another. As he stirred her emotions, he dropped to his knees to soap her legs, slipping his hand between them every once in a while to ensure he didn't miss an inch.

His muscles bunched, his thumb brushing her sensitive areas with a generous amount of finesse. The way he was tending to her forced her to call on every ounce of strength she could muster in an effort to keep her knees from failing. Her clit swelled and her breasts tightened, but tonight Cole's touch wasn't about sexual gratification. It was gentle, caring and tender, and no amount of armor could shield her from his protective hands or the way his touch produced a fullness in her heart. While sex with him was amazing, this sensitive side affected her on a whole new level and had her coming undone in front of him.

"Cole..." she said breathlessly. While she should be astonished at the things this man was making her feel, she wasn't.

He moved to the side to let the spray wash the soap and dirt from her body. "Yeah?"

"I want to wash you."

"Okay."

She reached for the soap and lathered her hands. Once sudsy, she set the bar aside and carefully brushed the mud from his face. He let loose a sigh and his head dropped forward when her hands moved to his chest. She moved his dog tags out of the way and spent a long time washing his upper body before turning her attention to the lower half.

"Turn around," she whispered.

Cole turned his back to her and braced his hands on the wall. Gemma lathered his cock, his backside and thighs before dropping to her knees to wash his calves. She slid back up his body and he sucked in a quick breath as her breasts scraped along his flesh.

"All done," she murmured and reached for the shampoo. Cole turned to her and his smile was soft when he grabbed the bottle from her hand to do his hair.

"The reach might be kind of hard for you." He washed his short hair quickly and gave her a playful roll of his eyes after rinsing. "Does everything have to be strawberry?"

Gemma laughed as he opened the glass door and reached into the cabinet to grab two towels. He tied his around his waist, then proceeded to pat her dry. Everything in his touch was so gentle, so caring, it had need clawing at her insides. Barely able to summon the strength to breathe, and craving the feel of him inside her again, she sucked in a quick, sharp breath.

When her chest heaved, he paused. "You okay?"

Not trusting herself to speak, she nodded. Hands skimming her curves, Cole wrapped the towel around her and guided her out of the shower stall. He picked her clear up off the floor and placed her on the counter before reaching for his clothes. He gave them a quick rinse in the sink, wrung them out and draped them over the shower to dry.

His warm scent filled her senses when he lifted her again to place her back on the floor. Dark eyes met hers and she stifled a yawn as the exhaustion of the night pulled at her.

"Come on," he murmured, his voice drowsy, sexy.

Lost in the moment, lost in him, she entwined her fingers through his and let him usher her out of the small bathroom. She fell into step beside him and Cole led her to the sofa without speaking. He sprawled out and pushed far against the back before reaching for her. She lowered herself and he shifted, dragging her hard against him. "Let's get some sleep," he murmured into her ear, his thumb lightly massaging the inside of her wrist.

He spooned her, her body fitting perfectly against his. His hands tightened around her waist and she listened to the steady beat of his strong heart. She diligently willed her own to slow down as a surge of warmth flooded her veins. Emotions pressed against her, forcing her to breathe slowly. Everything in his gentle touch had her yearning for so much more from him because, when it came to her feelings for Cole, there was nothing casual about them. She wanted the boy from her childhood in ways she'd never wanted another. But she didn't just want to be in his hands, she wanted to be in his heart.

Chapter Seven

Cole lay there for a long time holding Gemma until she fell asleep in his arms. Being with her like this reminded him of old times at the ranch when he'd hung out with Brandon. Equal measures of happiness and sadness hit him harder than flying pellets from an exploding IED and he worked to fight down the barrage of emotions before he became completely undone.

Once Gemma's breathing regulated to a soft, steady rhythm, Cole cleared his mind and let exhaustion take over. He awoke a few hours later to the brilliant morning sunlight streaming into the lounge, the storm long gone.

Gemma shifted beneath him, then turned until she was facing him. The towel he'd wrapped around her last night fell open to expose her skin—soft, lush, creamy skin his fingers itched to caress again. Sleepy eyes blinked up at him. She looked so warm and sexy all he could think about was pulling her on top of him and spending the rest of the day inside her.

"Good morning." She pushed her pelvis against his morning erection, which his cotton towel did little to hide.

Trying for casual, Cole brushed her hair from her face and her soft, throaty purr resonated through his body. "Sleep okay?"

She stretched and, if he wasn't mistaken, she'd purposely positioned her sex against his. There was a suggestive edge to her tone when she responded with, "Yeah, how about you?"

He stifled a tortured growl. "Pretty good."

"That was very sweet of you to help me last night."

There was that word *sweet* again. "It's what friends do," he said. "It's what Brandon would have wanted me to do." At the mention of her brother, she brushed her hand over the back of her neck and the look in her eyes turned serious.

"Cole?"

"Yeah?" His gut clenched. He didn't like the questioning look on her face, one that warned she wanted to talk—about him. If there was one person he didn't like to talk about it was himself.

"Now that you're back for good, what do you want?"

He shrugged. "No wars, no death, no loss."

She poked him in the chest. "But what do *you* want?"

"I want to work, train the dogs, help out at the motorcycle shop." She gave a small frown and he knew why. He'd purposely left *her* name off the list. Maybe that would show her he wasn't so sweet after all.

"Don't you want to settle down someday, start a family?"

Not liking where this conversation was going, or the way it had him wanting things that weren't his, he said, "Your staff will be here soon. We should get moving."

She gave a sigh. "How come you're so private and hate talking about yourself?"

He scrubbed his hand over his chin and, before he could think better of it, said, "It's a defense mechanism. It's no big deal."

She toyed with his dog chains. "What do you mean?"

Understanding she wasn't about to let this go, and not wanting to dredge up old memories, he hurried out with, "When

I was a kid, I learned not to draw attention to myself." He shrugged. "Like I said, it's no big deal."

She arched a brow and probed, the look on her face saying it was a big deal. To her. "Because of your father?"

Christ, he didn't want to be talking about this, didn't want her pity. "Yeah, he was a mean bastard."

"And?"

"And I had to be careful not to do or say anything that would draw attention to my family."

"What would have happened if you did?"

"He would have beaten the shit out of me." A noise sounded in his throat. "Then again, he didn't need a reason to kick my ass." There he'd said it, but he swore if he saw pity in her eyes, he'd never be able to look at her again.

Her hand went to his face and she traced the pattern of his jaw. When he dared to look at her he was relieved to see gentle understanding. "I'm sorry it was bad."

"I'm over it and we should go." With his hands biting into her hips, he looked past her shoulders. "Let's get you home."

"My first appointment will be here soon, so I might as well just stay."

"How about I take Stallone home with me, then. You can come by tonight after work to pick him up."

Before he could climb from the sofa, she dropped a soft kiss onto his mouth, one too full of emotion and passion. "Gemma," he murmured, his hands raking through her hair. "We can't keep...we can't keep sleeping together, okay?"

"Okay," she said, but he didn't miss the glimmer in her eyes. The bell over the front door jangled and she climbed to her feet. She gave him a tender smile full of promises as she adjusted her towel and made her way to her office to grab her scrubs.

Cole stomped into the bathroom and grabbed his clothes, which were still damp from the storm. Tugging them on anyway, he ran cold water over his face and pulled himself together before heading out to the front reception area.

Victoria's head went back with a start when she saw him coming from the back room. "Oh, I...you startled me." Her curious gaze panned his still-damp clothes.

He gestured with a nod toward the shelter. "Gemma and I came by last night to help Danielle with the dogs," he explained. "A few of them got spooked from the storm and took off. We had to rustle them back inside."

Victoria cringed and pressed her hand to her forehead. "I forgot to lock the doggy doors after you guys left yesterday."

The sound of heavy paws on the floor had Cole turning around. "Hey, boy," he said to Charlie as he pranced over, his new friend Stallone tight on his heels. He gave the dogs a rub, then straightened to see Gemma coming his way. The warm, pink flush on her cheeks and the way her silky hair swept against her shoulders had him wanting to drag her back into his arms and give her a proper good morning kiss. Long lashes blinked over tired eyes as she pushed her hair from her face, gathered it into her palms and tied it back in a professional manner.

Cole eyed her and knew she hadn't had enough sleep. "Are you going to be okay?"

"I'll be fine."

He smiled, understanding how strong of a woman she was. He lowered his voice and reached out and rubbed the hem of her scrubs between his fingers, unable to help himself. "Okay, the guys and I will be by shortly to round up a few of the dogs. Did you want me to bring you breakfast?"

She shook her head. "I'll grab something from the coffee shop next door." Her warm smile nearly disarmed him when she added, "But I appreciate the offer. It was sweet of you."

Knowing he needed to get out of there before his emotions got the better of him, he tapped his leg. "Let's go, boys."

He took care of the dogs and about an hour later, he decided to leave them both at his place for the morning while he met with the guys at the motorcycle shop.

"Hey," he said, pushing through the back door to find the others waiting for him.

Jack glared at him and he tried not to fidget under his shrewd glance. He met the man's dark eyes. *Don't look away. Don't look away.* He looked away. Shit. Under the pretense of studying the list of dogs they wanted to train first, he scooped a sheet of paper off the table.

"These are the ones we all agreed on?"

"You weren't here last night to have final word, so we agreed without you."

"Thunder and lightning," he explained. "The dogs got spooked and Gemma needed help rustling them up."

"Oh, is that what you were doing?" Jack asked.

"Yeah," he said, offering his friend his best hard-assed face. "Let's get out of here before the afternoon heat hits and the dogs need rest."

Thirty minutes later, after gathering the top five dogs with the right personalities for the job, they made their way to the base. They spent the morning working with them. Progress was slow, but these animals had huge potential. Buddy in particular—a mix between a collie and shepherd—was highly intelligent, if not a bit wily. He was always keeping an eye on Cole's hands, which was a very good sign.

Every now and then Cole would glance down the long gravel road and wonder if Gemma would be by to check on them. As he thought about the things they did inside that hangar the other day, he couldn't help but feel a sense of anticipation. Shit, hadn't he just said they couldn't sleep together anymore?

Josh stepped up to him. "What do you think of Ralph over there?"

Cole frowned. While Ralph was one of his first choices in dogs, he had him worried the most. The canine was intelligent and loyal enough, but he lacked direction. Clearly no one had ever given him the attention or training he needed just to be a loving pet. "I'm not ready to give up on him yet."

After talking technique with Josh, they all continued to work until midafternoon. With the sun high overhead, knowing the animals had had enough for the day, Josh gathered them in his truck and returned them to the shelter. Soon enough they'd be ready to be placed in the hands of soldiers, and free up space for Gemma. Cole went back to the shop with Jack to help out at the front counter while his friend worked on repairs out back. As dinner hour approached, he switched the sign over the door and shouted out to Jack that he was leaving.

The night air was cooler now that the storm had passed and as he walked the short distance to his condo, he decided a couple pit stops were in order. He grabbed a bottle of wine and made his way into one of the many restaurants lining the street. Once armed with food and drink, he hurried home. He was anxious to hear about Gemma's day and in turn tell her about the progress they were making.

He pulled the food out of the bag, stuck the wine in the fridge to chill, and was reaching for the plates when the dogs started barking. Clearly they were aware of Gemma's presence long before he was.

Cole hurried to his door and pulled it open. The second he found Gemma standing on his stoop his heart beat a little quicker.

She gave him a big smile before bending to pet the dogs. She rubbed Stallone's ears and he pushed against her. "I hope old Stallone here didn't give you any trouble."

"Stallone's a good old boy."

She tugged on his collar. "Are you ready to go home and get some dinner?"

"I already fed him."

"Oh," she said, surprise apparent in her expression as she stood to face him. "What did you feed him?"

Cole knew as well as any dog owner that you couldn't switch up an animal's food without causing digestion problems and Stallone's diet was different than Charlie's, which meant he had to have his own food. "I grabbed some of his food from your pantry."

"You were in my place?"

"I hope you don't mind."

"No, not at all. I just...how did you get in?"

He pulled a key from his pocket. "The spare key you keep under your mat."

She gave him a sheepish look and held her hands up in surrender. "I don't want to hear the lecture."

"I don't want to give you one. Just keep it here at my place from now on, okay?"

Her eyes lit with amusement. "Oh, and how can I trust that you won't sneak into my condo in the middle of the night and try to ravish me when I'm asleep?"

"You can't," he teased in return.

"Well then, I guess you can keep it." She gave Cole a devious wink and reached for Stallone. "Let's go, boy. I'm anxious to get home and get to bed early tonight."

"I fed Stallone and thought I'd feed you too."

"You want to feed me?" She shot him a curious glance. "Since when did you become domestic?"

"It's all ready if you're hungry, and I have wine chilling."

"Ah, now I see how this is playing out. First you keep my key and now you're trying to lure me with alcohol." She looked past his shoulders and inhaled the scents coming from the kitchen. "I must say, this night is shaping up to be a good one."

Cole laughed and grabbed her hand. "Come on. Let's eat. I want to tell you all about the training today."

He led her into the kitchen and her stomach rumbled as she inhaled again. "Mmm, smells so good."

"It's pasta." He rolled one shoulder. "With mushroom sauce."

"My favorite kind." She smiled. "Like I said, sweet."

She moved past him and made her way to the kitchen. "Cole, this looks amazing. I had no idea you could cook."

This time he gave the sheepish grin. "I picked it up."

Gemma laughed. "Still, I appreciate the thoughtfulness."

"Grab the wine." He gestured to the fridge as he reached for the glasses. "Then have a seat while I make our plates up. First I want to hear about your day and how the fundraising is going, then I want to tell you how training went."

A few minutes later, Gemma lowered herself into one of the chairs and took a sip of white wine. As she watched Cole divvy up the pasta and bread she began. "Well, today I found out for certain that we're going to have a banquet in Dallas."

Cole carried the plates over and placed them on the table. "Oh yeah?"

She nodded. "It will be in a couple of weeks. The event planners are putting it together and feel that if I expand my area it will bring in new blood."

"And new blood means new money." Cole handed out forks and knives and sat next to her. She went on to explain the details of the event and as he listened to her something inside him hitched. He couldn't help but notice how normal this all felt, how right it felt to be sitting with her at the end of the night talking about their days.

"Okay, enough about me," she said, her eyes alive with curiosity. "I want to hear about the training today."

Cole told her all about Buddy, Ralph and the others while they ate and drank. Once he finished relaying every last detail he noticed the way she was smiling at him.

"Why are you looking at me like that?" he asked.

"Because it's nice to see you fired up about something again. You really do love working with these dogs, don't you?"

He gave a shrug like it was nothing. "Yeah."

"Is that why you became a bomb expert, so you could work with the K9 unit?"

Cole got quiet for a moment, his gut tightening as he thought about the real reason he opted to work with dogs. "No," he said, that one word almost a whisper as his mind raced for something else to talk about.

Her hand reached out to touch his, and she gave a gentle squeeze. "Cole?"

He wasn't sure what suddenly possessed him to say it. Maybe it was the good food, the fine wine or the easy conversation. Then again maybe it had more to do with the way Gemma felt so right in his place, the way her hand felt so comforting on his. But against his better judgment he found himself saying, "It was because of you, Gems."

He listened to the sound of her throat working as she swallowed. "Because of me?"

He stared at his empty plate and toyed with his fork. "You loved your horses and dogs so much, and when I went away, leaving you and your family, working with the dogs somehow helped me feel closer to you and those I left behind."

Cole tilted his chin, and when his gaze met with blue eyes full of emotion, everything inside him twisted into knots. He wasn't sure who moved first. But the next thing he knew Gemma was in his arms and he was kissing her like a man starved for affection, a man hungering for much more than just sex.

"Gemma," he said, his voice low and rough as warning bells went off inside him. Jesus, he was getting in so deep he'd soon need a compass to find his way out.

She locked her arms around his neck. "Don't think, Cole, just enjoy."

He exhaled slowly and, with primitive need ruling his actions, he scooped her up and carried her to his room. He gently tossed her on the bed. With her body lit only by the glow of the moon outside his window, Cole shut his mind to everything except the heat between them.

Deciding to simply savor the moment, he stared at the woman on his bed, taking note of the warmth in her eyes and the way her body beckoned his touch. He pulled his shirt off and kicked his pants away, the soft rustle of his clothes the only audible sound in the room.

Her glance met his, then trailed lower to roam over his nakedness. He took in her sexy bedroom eyes, as well as the color blooming high on her cheeks. As she welcomed him to her body, he knew he was in so much fucking trouble.

A tremble moved through him and the compulsion to touch her prompted him into action. He climbed on top of her and trailed kisses around her jaw, going lower and lower on her neck. When he caught her unique scent, the intoxicating tang of her arousal, he closed his eyes in sweet agony.

When he opened them again, her hands wrapped around his shoulder and she pulled him to her mouth. She kissed him long and hard, before rolling out from underneath him. She pinned him to the bed and straddled him. His hands went to her shirt.

"Take it off."

In one smooth movement she removed her shirt and tossed it on the floor. Her bra quickly followed. Cole groaned at the sight of her beautiful breasts and went up on his elbows to draw one perfect nipple into his mouth. He turned his attention to the other. He still couldn't get enough of her.

He fell back onto his pillow. "Now these," he said, his fingers unleashing her drawstring.

She shimmied off his lap, made quick work of her pants and panties. Naked, she climbed back on top of him.

As she straddled his hips, he cupped her breasts as she lifted herself to grip his cock in her hands. She positioned him and when his crown breached her opening, he brushed his thumbs over her nipples. "You are so beautiful."

She wiggled her hips, ready to impale herself on him, but he grabbed her hips and took control of her movements. He lowered her slowly, offering only an inch at a time. His slow seduction earned him a scowl.

"Cole," she murmured, her voice a low, anguished whisper.

"Don't worry, baby. I'm going to give you what you want."

He pushed deeper, giving her inch by inch and loving the way she was squirming, so hot for him.

"So good." She undulated against him, until he burrowed his entire cock inside her.

She began moving, rocking, taking what her body needed. When her fingers went to her clit his blood pressure spiked. She threw her head back and her breasts swayed as she rubbed herself. Cole was certain it was the most erotic sight he'd ever seen.

His balls tightened, the crescendo of their union pushing him to the edge far too quickly. He held her waist, and followed her movement with his hands as she rode his cock with wild abandonment. Cole could feel longing build with every caress, his orgasm mounting rapidly. She leaned forward, her hands racing over his body, the feel of skin on skin robbing him of his next breath.

He brushed his thumb over her clit as his cock stroked deep. She cried out, her lids fluttering as she gave herself over to the sensation. Jesus, she was so responsive to him. So fucking responsive.

"Oh fuck, Gems," he murmured when her hot cream poured over him. Their moans of pleasure merged as he powered upward. Her heat scorched him and he clenched his jaw, fearing he was seeking more than just sexual release as he strove to be deeper. His cock throbbed inside her, his muscles trembling, eager to let go.

She bent forward and pressed her lips to his. As she coaxed his tongue out, sensations ripped through him. He gripped her hips harder, no longer able to hold on. "Gems," he murmured, releasing everything he had inside her.

A moment later she collapsed on his chest. Cole worked to get his panting under control as moisture fused their bodies together.

"My God that was good." Her lips scraped his neck, her long, silky curls tumbling in disarray over his shoulders and sheets. She inched back, and the soft, sexy smile on her face made his heart pound harder. She opened her mouth to say something else when ringing from the other room interrupted her.

The smile fell from her face as she glanced at the clock and took note of the time.

"That would be my mother." She exhaled slowly. "I'd better get that before she sends out a search party."

Cole flipped off his sheets. "I'll get it." He hurried to the other room, grabbed her purse and brought it back. Gemma rifled through it as he climbed back under the sheets. He flopped down on his pillow and drove his arm under his head.

Gemma answered the call. "Hello, Mother."

Cole listened to the muffled voice on the other end, and Gemma pinched the bridge of her nose. "I'm fine, really. I was visiting Cole. He took care of Stallone for the day."

She went silent for a moment and Cole cast her a sideways glance as she listened to her mother.

"Stallone is fine, and no, I already have an escort." Cole listened to her mother's muffled words on the other end, as Gemma briefly closed her eyes. "Please tell me you didn't set this whole event in motion so you could introduce the two of us."

Cole's gut clenched, a surge of possessive emotions coiling through him as he listened to the one-sided conversation. Which rich benefactor did her mother wanted Gemma on the arm of this time around?

"No, Mother, Cole is taking me."

Cole eyed her suspiciously and she covered the phone and whispered, "Sorry."

She exchanged a few more words with her mother, then exhaled slowly, staring at some distant spot on the wall. Her mood was pensive after she hung up.

He touched her chin to bring her focus back to his. "Where exactly am I taking you?"

"To the banquet." Gemma's fingers tightened in the sheets and she screwed her nose up apologetically. "But you don't have to. I said that to get my mother off my back. She's been trying to get me to do an event in Dallas for a long time and now I'm beginning to suspect she's trying to get me there for other reasons."

"Like what? What does she want?"

"She wants to set me up with the son of some rich banker she knows."

Oddly enough Cole began to feel a little angry that Audrey thought he was good enough to watch over Gemma, but not good enough for her. "What do you want?"

"I want her to stop trying to fix me up."

"Why don't you tell her that?"

"I have but you know how insistent she is when she sets her mind to something."

"She's not the only one. You're also a girl who goes after what you want and doesn't let anyone push her around."

Her face softened and he felt something in her give. "It's just that she worries about me. I'm all she has now." Her hand rubbed the back of her neck.

"Come here." He pulled her to him as his heart ached for her. He held her for a long time, twirling her hair between his fingers. "I'll take you."

"I can't ask you to do that. I know you're not comfortable—"

"I'll take you," he said firmly, because the thought of her attending with another man, even if that man was mother-approved and he wasn't, had his blood boiling. As he stroked her hair, she snuggled against him. Cole fought valiantly to suppress the things this incredible woman made him feel, because when it came to Gemma it was getting harder and harder to separate sex and emotions.

Chapter Eight

Gemma's shoes clicked a steady beat on the shelter's floor as she finished checking on the last animal. Adoptions had been going well for the last month, and Cole said he was making great progress with the dogs in the field. If the funding she needed to expand came through at tomorrow night's banquet she'd never have to turn any animals away.

Feeling a sense of elation, she made her way to the reception area, a new spring to her step. Of course, that was probably because she'd been having the best sex of her life. Since that first night she'd eaten dinner with Cole a couple weeks ago, they'd been spending all their time together. They shared meals every evening, walked the dogs afterward, and the nights were usually capped off by a mind-blowing round of sex.

As she thought about the way Cole cared for her in bed, she knew his touch was anything but casual, but there was still a part of him he kept closed off to her. Even though she was in deep, had laid herself bare to Cole numerous times, he continued to maintain a degree of emotional separation. Which once again had her wondering about his demons and the secrets he held close.

"Hey, Victoria," she said, checking the clock. The staff had gone to lunch already, and Gemma's next appointment was still an hour away. Both she and Victoria had some time to kill until then. "I'm heading to the field to bring lunch and check on progress, would you like to come?"

Victoria's eyes lit and she was already grabbing her purse. "Like you even have to ask."

Gemma locked the clinic and grabbed a stack of sandwiches and drinks at the café next door for the guys. Arms full, they hurried back to her place, where her car sat in the driveway. Less than fifteen minutes later, they drove the long, winding road to the base.

She turned to see Victoria, who was watching Josh with bright-eyed enthusiasm as he played catch with one of the dogs.

"You be careful with that one," Gemma teased.

Victoria turned to her. "What do you know about him?"

"He's been through some rough times and doesn't appear to be the settling-down type, but he's definitely one of the good guys."

"Well, who says I'm looking to settle down?" She shrugged and gave a mischievous grin. "Maybe, like you, I'm just looking to have a little fun, enjoy it while it lasts and take away a few good memories."

Suddenly an apprehensive knot tightened in her gut. She wanted so much more than that with Cole, except while they were having fun together, they never talked long-term. In fact, Cole seemed to go out of his way to avoid it, which had her worrying their relationship could very well play out the way Victoria had just described it. Before she could give it more thought, Cole came out from the hangar. When he saw her, he waved and made his way over.

She climbed from the car and handed him a sandwich. Hoping to keep the worry from her voice she said, "Lunch is here."

"I'll deliver the rest to the others," Victoria said, a devious glint in her eyes as she took the stack of food and drinks and made her way over to the guys.

Once she was out of earshot, Cole narrowed those perceptive eyes of his and she knew she could never hide anything from him. "You okay?"

"Yeah," she said. "Just thinking about the banquet tomorrow night and hoping my speech goes over well."

"I'm sure it will be fine."

Redirecting the conversation, she said, "Why don't you show me how Ralph is making out."

Cole frowned. "He's a great dog, but he still lacks direction."

"Let's go see him."

Gemma made her way into the hangar and for the next half hour Cole went through the exercises with the dogs. When he finished, Gemma bent to pet Ralph, his long tail beating rigorously against her leg in response.

"He sure is a smart one."

"But he has a mind of his own. After identifying the right box, he's supposed to sit, bark and wag. Instead he wants to dig for the device because he knows it's dangerous."

"Ah, that's why you have a soft spot for him."

"What do you mean?"

"He's a protector, like you."

Cole frowned. "But the way he protects could get someone killed."

"How?"

"If he digs at a device in the field, it could very well explode."

Gemma crinkled her nose. "Maybe he'd be better served as someone's watch dog."

Cole arched a brow. "How long has he been in the shelter?"

"You're right." She blew a disgruntled breath. "No one is in a hurry to adopt a mature dog."

"Like you said, everyone wants a puppy, and I'm not ready to give up on him. Besides, if I can train a wily guy like him, I'm sure I can train any dog. It would sure as hell go a long way in helping the animals, the soldiers and your cause."

Her heart warmed and she was about to go up on her toes to kiss him when Jack poked his head in. Cole stiffened and inched away from her, his actions telling. Even though she wanted to scream their affair from the rooftop, he didn't want anyone to know what was going on behind closed doors.

"Thanks for lunch, Gemma," Jack said.

Gemma's heart sank a little. "Anytime."

"What time will you be dropping Stallone off?"

Originally her plans had been to shelter Stallone at the clinic while she was away in Dallas, but when Jack found out he jumped at the chance to watch him for her. "Right after work if that's okay."

"See you then." With that he disappeared around the side of the building.

She stole a glance at her watch. "I need to get back."

"I'll walk you out."

As they made their way back to her car, her mind went back to what Victoria had said about their relationship. She wanted to talk to him and get him to open up to her on a personal level, to figure out what was going on inside his mind. Except this wasn't the time or place.

"What time are you leaving for Dallas?"

Gemma had hoped to share a ride there with Cole. The long drive would give them an opportunity to talk. But she had to go earlier and oversee some last-minute arrangements.

"Right after work. I'm catching a drive with my mother." She rolled her eyes. "I was going to take my own car but she insisted I go with her. That way I can't escape when she starts telling me about all the bachelors who will be attending and what great marriage material they'd make."

She waited for a reaction to her bachelor comment, but instead he just said, "I guess I'll see you tomorrow night."

"Are you sure you don't mind coming?"

"I said I'd take you, Gems, and I don't—"

She held her hands up to cut him off. "I know, I know you're a soldier and soldiers don't go back on their word." She grinned, brushed her hand along the back of her neck and said, "I can't tell you how many times Brandon said that to me. He prided himself on his honor." As soon as the words left her mouth, Cole's face tightened warily and he gripped his dog tags like they were his lifeline. Gemma stared at him. What had she said to spook him?

"I gotta go," he said and turned and disappeared back into the hangar.

After Gemma fought down an uneasy feeling, she and Victoria made their way back to the clinic. The rest of the afternoon sped by. After work she dropped Stallone off with Jack, and before she knew it her mother's chauffeur was outside her condo, ready to drive her to Dallas.

She grabbed her overnight bag and as she made her way down the steps she spotted Cole in his window. She gave a small wave but couldn't fight down the feeling something was very wrong. Very wrong indeed.

She had no time to consider it further, because when she climbed into the back seat with her mother and the car set into motion, her mother started in on her.

"So, Gemma," she began with an efficient clap of her hands that rattled the gold bracelets linked around her wrist as she got right to the point, "since I haven't seen you in ages, I'm glad we have this time alone. I've been eager to talk to you about a few of the men who will be at the function tomorrow night. I know Marie Johnson and Sandra Phillips will be attending with their sons who are both rich, successful, eligible bachelors. They're very interested in supporting your cause."

As her mother pushed, Gemma could feel a headache beginning at the base of her neck. She shifted on the leather seat, tucking her sundress under her legs. As gently as she could under the circumstances she said, "I'm sure they're nice men, Mother, but I'm not sure if they're my type."

Her mother arched a disapproving brow, her blue eyes narrowing to mere slits. "Are you telling me rich, successful men who want to help your cause aren't your type?"

Gemma folded her hands in her lap and glanced out the window to watch the city streets fly by. "That's not what I mean."

"Then what do you mean?"

Feeling a little angry that her mother thought only wealthy men with the right pedigree made good marriage material, she turned back to her and said, "There are lots of men who want to help my cause and they're not rich. But that doesn't mean they're not successful, or good men."

"Ah, I see." Her mother pursed perfectly painted lips and folded her ring-clad fingers in her lap. If Gemma wasn't mistaken she thought she caught a smug look on her face before she said, "Tell me what's been going on with Cole."

Unable to help herself, and wanting to talk about Cole, Gemma began rehashing everything he'd told her over the last few nights. She went on for hours explaining the work he was doing, even telling her mother about Ralph and how Cole was determined to shape him into a service dog. She was droning on about him, but she couldn't seem to help herself. The guy was deep under her skin and pretty much consumed her every thought.

When she finished speaking, her mother sat there staring at her.

"What?" Gemma asked, suddenly uncomfortable under her mother's scrutiny.

"Tell me something," she said, unmasked hurt in her eyes. "If you have no problem with Cole and the others helping you, why is it you shun my help?" She waved her hand toward the hotel as the car approached. "These benefits are wonderful, Gemma, but the expenses associated with putting them together are high and the profits that go toward your shelter are low. I invest in many charities, why won't you let me invest in yours?"

As her mother's words bounced around inside her head like a rubber chew toy, the driver pulled off the highway. Her mother leaned forward to speak to him, saving Gemma from having to answer.

A few minutes later, the driver pulled up in front of a regal hotel, climbed from the front and opened the door for them both. Gemma stepped out. Even though the warm air hit like a slap to the face, Gemma was happy to escape the confines of the vehicle and find a moment of solitude in her room. With a headache brewing, she took a few moments to compose herself before she met with the event planner to go over the final arrangements in the ballroom.

She was supposed to meet her mother at the bar but hated the thought of another interrogation. Instead she excused herself and made her way back to her room. She took a warm shower and plunked down on her cushy bed. She lay there staring at the ceiling for a long while, wondering if she would hear from Cole tonight. As her mind drifted toward him, she couldn't shake the feeling that something dark and destructive was going on inside of him. She picked the phone up to call, but the uneasy feeling mushrooming inside of her had her putting it back down again.

Deciding a good night's sleep was in order before she faced a busy day, she turned her attention to her cell phone. She set the alarm and placed it on the nightstand. After tossing and turning for hours, she finally fell into a fitful sleep.

When her alarm clock went off, she groaned and stretched out her tired limbs. Even though she wanted to roll over and go back to sleep she still had a lot to do before the night's events. She shoved off her blankets and checked her phone once again, only to find Cole hadn't tried to contact her.

Pushing down the disappointment, she climbed to her feet, showered and busied her mind with activities until nighttime was upon her. With the event about to begin in less than an hour, she hurried to her room and took extra care in her appearance, leaving her hair down the way Cole liked it.

She applied the last bit of her makeup and finished off with her red lipstick. Satisfied with the outcome, she climbed into her brand new strapless black cocktail dress and stood back to give herself a once-over in the mirror. As she checked herself from the back, her phone rang. She nearly tripped in her too-high heels when she ran to grab it, but her heart sank when she saw it was the event planner. They spoke briefly, then Gemma made her way down to the foyer.

Guests were already starting to arrive and Gemma held her hand out to greet each and every one of them personally. Plastering on a smile and trying not to worry about Cole's whereabouts or why he hadn't called last night, she spoke to the benefactors, thanking them for coming. Of course, deep in her heart she knew she shouldn't fret too much about him. Cole was a stand-up guy who made good on his word, which once again had her wondering why he'd acted oddly yesterday when she'd said as much.

Once the majority of the guests had arrived and wandered into the lounge for cocktails, her mother came up to her. Worry moved into her eyes as she scanned the lobby. "I thought Cole was escorting you."

"He is." She glanced at her watch. "He must be running late."

Her mother continued to go on about the importance of her having a date and how she should have let her fix her up with one of the eligible bachelors from her country club. But her litany faded to a dull drone because coming through the front entrance was none other than the most handsome man to cross the hotel's threshold. Dressed in a midnight black suit that fit to perfection, with his hair freshly cut and his face recently shaved, he closed the distance between them. The dark intensity in his gaze had her stomach knotting once again and her intuition telling her there really was something wrong.

"Gemma," he greeted, his hand going to her lower back. "You look beautiful." He glanced at her mother, who was staring up at him in frank approval. "Sorry I'm late," he said, bending to drop a kiss onto her mother's cheek. "I had to get a new suit and alterations took longer than expected."

As he guided Gemma through the foyer, she noted the way all eyes turned on them, the benefactors appraising her date every bit as much as they were judging her. Nor did she miss the way her body was reacting from his close proximity.

He gave a humorless laugh, put his mouth close to her ear and, in a self-deprecating manner, said, "I know I'm not the son of a rich benefactor, or what these people consider a respected suitor, but I'll do my best not to embarrass you."

Her heart thudded in her chest because that somber laugh had her realizing something very important—not only did he feel uncomfortable in her world, he felt these people were out of his league.

"Cole," she began, lowering her voice to match his as she grabbed his hand to stop him. He turned to face her, and dipped his head. "Within ten minutes of finding out what was important to me, you were acting on it, rounding up the guys and finding a way to help me, the dogs and all of America," she rushed out. "Sure these guys open their wallets, and I appreciate that, believe me I do, but none of them took action the way you did, helping me the only way you knew how. That means more to me than anything, and believe me, Cole, you're in a league of your own here."

An emotion she couldn't identify passed over his eyes, then they darkened, a volatile storm brewing beneath the surface. Gemma swallowed and wondered what was going on with him.

The ballroom doors opened and everyone filed into the elegant, dimly lit room to take a seat. Cole grabbed a glass of champagne from the waiter when he walked by and swallowed it down in one gulp.

Looking out of place as benefactors milled about, he glanced around. Gemma nodded toward the podium and gave him an apologetic smile. "I have to go up there. But I won't be long." She hesitated and asked, "Are you going to be okay?"

His jaw tightened. "I'm fine, Gemma," he said, even though she got the sense he was anything but.

Her mother stepped up to them. "Cole, darling, sit next to me. We need to talk. You promised you'd come to dinner and I've yet to see you."

"Sorry about that, Audrey." Cole pulled out a chair for her and she smoothed down her black satin dress before sitting. Her rings glistened in the light as she tapped the seat beside him. "Come. Sit. Let's talk." Cole sank into the chair, and Gemma's mother went on to say, "Frank will be back from his business meeting tomorrow night. He'd love to see you. Say you'll come by."

"I'll come by," he promised.

"Gemma, you too," she insisted.

Gemma excused herself and maneuvered around the tables as the staff delivered the first course of the five-course meal planned for tonight's event. A hush fell over the crowd as the emcee introduced her and she took to the podium to begin her speech.

As she spoke about her cause, she looked out over the audience, but her gaze kept going to Cole. Everything in the intense way he was looking at her, his dark eyes unreadable, had butterflies taking flight in her stomach.

Her mother waved some man over, and she didn't miss the way Cole glared at him as he sat down at their table. As they exchanged words Gemma couldn't hear, Gemma stumbled over her own, completely thrown off her game. With the audience watching her carefully, she worked to get herself together. Normally she was poised in front of a crowd, but with her thoughts on Cole and the commotion that seemed to be going on at their table, she couldn't quite focus on her speech.

Cole's eyes met hers again and she sucked in a sharp breath, grasping for her rehearsed words as they abandoned her. She gripped the podium until her knuckles turned white and she willed her mind to settle. Cole leaned in, spoke to her mother and a second later he was standing. For a moment she thought he was leaving the room. Blood pounded through her veins when he began to make his way to the podium, coming to her rescue yet again.

Their gazes locked as he came close and she assumed he was there to escort her offstage before she made a bigger fool of herself, but when he stood at the podium beside her, her heart turned over in her chest.

"Cole," she squeaked out. "What are you doing?"

"I've got this, Gemma."

Before she could say another word, he adjusted the microphone. A quick flash of panic clutched her as she watched him. Why was he doing this when it was hard for him to put himself in the public eye? He hated to draw attention to himself like this. She could only imagine it would dredge up memories that could only be painful, memories from his childhood and memories from the battlefield? The truth was she'd rather ask her parents for help than to put Cole through this. But as she watched him, she knew the reason behind his actions and the answer to her questions. He was doing this for her, so she wouldn't have to ask her parents for funding.

He cleared his throat and began. "I'm US Army Specialist Cole Sullivan, a tactical explosive expert and detector dog handler with the Company B, 2nd Battalion, 12th Infantry Regiment, 4th Brigade Combat Team, 4th Division Infantry." He paused for a moment and drew in a fueling breath before continuing. "When I was overseas I worked closely with a service dog. His name is Charlie, and he's not here with me tonight because he's at a sleepover." Even though it wasn't meant to be funny, the audience laughed and there was nothing Gemma could do to swallow down the cantaloupe-sized lump pushing into her throat.

Once the sound settled, he continued. "Charlie isn't just my dog or my comrade in the field. He is my friend. My confidante. And most importantly, he is my family." A hush fell over the room and Cole gripped the podium harder. "Charlie has been with me for two years now and when we were overseas and all looked bleak, he was there to support me, unconditionally. To a soldier, one who is away from everyone and everything they hold close, the love and loyalty from their canine is the only thing that keeps them going sometimes."

Gemma watched emotions move over the faces in the crowd. As Cole commanded the room, his words quietly powerful and genuinely passionate, it occurred to her how deeply in love she was with him.

He continued to talk about the unexploded explosive ordinances and how he and his comrades were personally training the dogs for the safety of all Americans. As he spoke, he was funny, charming and sincere, and within seconds he had the audience enthralled, each and every person hanging off his every last word.

He choked on his words but quickly recovered as he talked about his comrades, those who were soldiering on and those he'd lost, both human and canine, and how this cause was a tribute to them all. His hand closed over his chest, gripping at his dog tags, and Gemma knew he was thinking about Brandon as he stole a quick glance at her.

He turned back to the audience. "With your funding and my expertise, we'll be able to train canines and get them into the hands of our soldiers. So you see, expanding the shelter isn't just about saving unwanted dogs, it's also about saving soldiers." He paused and his voice wavered slightly when he added, "In more ways than one." The audience started to clap but Cole held his hand up to stop them. "In closing I'd like to say that if I haven't convinced you to invest, I'm not above siccing Charlie on you until you see things my way."

With that the audience laughed and chairs scraped across the floor as they stood to applaud.

Cole walked away, and when he moved into the shadows, Gemma said a few quick closing words, handed the microphone off to the emcee, then went after him.

"Cole," she said breathlessly, her throat closing when she caught up to him. He turned to face her and she wanted to thank him but words would never be enough for what he did for her.

He looked past her shoulders toward the door. "I gotta get out of here, Gemma."

Cole raked his hands through his hair and when his gaze met hers, her heart nearly seized. Cole Sullivan was the toughest guy she knew, but tonight his bravado had been stripped bare. In fact, those big, brown, puppy dog eyes of his looked a little sad, and a whole lot lost.

He'd once told her everyone needed someone sometimes, but Cole was always giving, never taking, and tonight was a prime example. He'd run to her rescue once again, no matter the cost to him, no matter how many personal demons it resurrected. But no one had been running to him, and from the vulnerability in his eyes tonight, she knew he was in need of rescuing.

There was much more going on with him than met the eye, yet she'd been so caught up in her own wants and desires, so busy going after what she wanted she hadn't stopped to consider what he needed, what was best for Cole.

As she considered the way she'd been acting with him, she mentally kicked herself. She'd been behaving like the young, impetuous girl from her youth. And while she'd always have that side of her, she was also a grown woman and it was time to start acting like one. After everything Cole had ever done for her, he deserved at least that much from her. His whole life had been about shouldering responsibility and taking care of others. Tonight she wanted to show him it was okay for someone else to take care of him.

"Come on," she whispered, knowing there would be time for talking later. Right now Cole needed to take without giving. She needed him to release the tension in his body and let go of a few of the demons haunting him.

Cole swallowed and the raw emotions in his eyes when he said, "I should go, Gemma," hit like a punch to the stomach.

"The only place you're going is to my room, with me." She grabbed his hand to prevent him from fleeing. He needed and deserved much more from her, even if he didn't yet know it.

She led him to the elevators and, once inside, she slipped her arm around his waist, in desperate need of his intimate contact at all times. Looking antsy and agitated, he was about to say something but closed his mouth again, his brows furrowing together.

When they reached her floor, she led him to her room, and guided him inside. He stood there, his dark eyes looking so lost and haunted that her heart ached for him.

She nudged him backward until he fell on the bed. She dropped down in front of him and pressed her lips to his. She kissed him with passion and hunger, eager to make this night about him, eager to take care of him for a change. Her hands went to his suit jacket and she slipped it off his shoulder, then undid his shirt. Once she had his upper body bare, she turned her attention to his pants. She unhooked the button but he gripped her arm to stop her.

"What are you doing?" he asked, emotions thickening his voice.

She blinked up at him. "I'm taking care of you."

Expression pained, he whispered, "You don't have to do that. Not for me."

"I know I don't have to, but did you ever think I wanted to?"

"Gemma—"

"You know, Cole, everyone needs someone sometimes. You once told me that yourself."

"But you don't have—" She dipped her hand inside his pants and captured his cock in her palm. He threw his head back and let loose a tortured groan as she gently stroked the length of him, until he was hard and swollen and ready for her mouth.

As she continued to caress him her other hand went to his zipper. She drew it down and unleashed his hard cock from his shorts. Cole opened his mouth to say something, but when she bent forward to draw him into her mouth, his words of protest were lost on a moan.

"Fuck, Gems."

She drew him in as deep as she could and he began trembling all over. Cole threaded his fingers through her hair, his hands following the motions. She ran her hands up his legs and he began to jut his hips forward, pushing into her mouth, taking what he needed from her.

"Jesus...I..."

He began pumping, rocking into her, his breathing becoming labored, his hands gripping her hair harder as a groan caught in his throat.

She inched back and stroked him with her hands as she met his eyes. "I've got you, Cole," she assured him. "This time I've got you."

When she drew him back into her mouth, he took deep, gulping breaths and began moving, pushing deep. Everything in what they were doing was far more intimate than anything they'd done to date. He pulled her hair back to watch and she glanced up at him. When their eyes met, something important passed between them, and she guessed he knew every bit as much as she did this was about so much more than sex.

Tension raced through his body, coming to a peak. A moment later, his body jerked and he gripped her head to pull her off. When she refused to move, he fisted her hair and cursed out loud. She cupped his balls and could feel blood rushing through his veins.

"Gems," he bit out, his cock spasming around her tongue moments before his liquid heat filled her mouth.

She drank him all in, and stayed burrowed between his thighs until his breathing returned to normal. When she inched back, he brushed his thumb over her mouth. She nearly sobbed from the emotions and tenderness filling his dark eyes.

With his pants half off he shimmied backward and collapsed on the pillow. His voice dropped to a whisper as he reached for her. "Come here." She climbed in beside him, needing him to hold her while she held him in return. He wrapped his arm around her, his hand going to her zipper. Cole wasn't a guy who took without giving.

She shook her head and pressed against him. Tonight she didn't want a physical union, she wanted an emotional one. "This is all about you. Not me."

Silence hung for a long time, then he finally broke it by saying, "Gemma," but she silenced him with a kiss. She didn't want anything to break this profound moment between them.

Gemma snuggled in tight and Cole squeezed her so hard it was nearly impossible to fill her lungs. Both lost in their own thoughts, they stayed that way until they fell asleep and her morning wake-up call roused them.

She blinked her eyes open to see Cole and her heart beat a little faster. Dear God, how could she not love a man who wanted to protect her, a man who put his own feelings and best interests aside for her? A man who'd rather face a firing squad than a room full of benefactors yet did it anyway? For her.

While he might not have been her first lover like she'd hoped at seventeen, there was no denying she wanted him to be her last. This thing between them went well beyond casual sex. When he blinked his tortured eyes open and caught her watching him, she wondered what it was going to take for him to acknowledge it too.

Chapter Nine

Cole put down his razor and stared at his reflection in the bathroom mirror. He thought about canceling on dinner tonight, but after everything Brandon and Gemma's parents had done for him, he definitely owed them a visit. Hell, he owed them a lot more than that.

He suspected, however, they'd take one look at him and Gemma and know what they'd been doing for the last month. And while both Audrey and Frank loved him like a son, from the way Gemma's mother was pushing wealthy, upscale men on her only daughter, he knew they weren't keen on loving him like a son-in-law.

Son-in-law.

Shit, where the hell had that thought come from? If Brandon were here he'd be kicking his ass. Rightfully so. Cole dropped his razor back into its case and his hands went to his dog tags. Guilt ate him up inside to think how he'd been dishonoring his best friend's dying wish. He wasn't about to swallow the emotions down. He damn well deserved to feel like a traitorous prick.

He finished up in the bathroom, then glanced at his watch. Gemma had to do a home visit, to check on the young girl who'd recently adopted a puppy. She'd asked him to come along, but he declined and told her he'd meet her at her folks' place. The thoughts of seeing that young girl with her family, all happy and loving, might be more than he could take right now.

With a few minutes to spare, he took Charlie out for a walk. When he returned home, Charlie curled up on his bed and Cole made his way to his bike. The air was still hot and a ride might help cool his body and clear his head, not to mention blow the scent of a well-fucked guy off his skin before he sat down to dinner with Gemma's folks.

He drove across town and by the time he reached Audrey and Frank's upscale apartment, Gemma had already arrived. He pulled his bike in behind her car and made his way inside. When he reached the door and was about to knock, Gemma pulled it open. Her smile was so warm and welcoming, it nearly brought him to his knees. His mind instantly rewound to last night and the way she'd taken care of him. There was no doubt this woman was clawing past his defenses without even trying. The sheer intimacy in what she did for him last night, taking him into her mouth and caring for him when he was feeling a little raw and exposed made his heart ache. Jesus, she was so kind and compassionate, giving without taking. It had him wanting things he simply couldn't have, things that weren't his to have.

She went up on her toes and lifted her mouth to his. Instead of giving her what she wanted, he placed a kiss on her cheek. He didn't miss the disappointment in her eyes or the way that sadness in her baby blues cut right to his core.

"Cole," Audrey said, breaking the tension between them as she stepped up beside Gemma. "Come in, come in." She led him into the living room where Frank sat on the sofa, nursing a drink.

"Cole," Frank greeted, standing to wrap his arms around him. "How have you been, son?"

Cole returned the hug, his heart squeezing in his too-tight chest not only because the man who'd become his surrogate father had called him son, but also because one look at Frank reminded him so much of Brandon.

He cleared his throat. "Things are good, Frank."

"Good, good, come have a drink with me."

Frank poured a generous amount of dark rum into a tumbler and handed it to him. Cole took a swig and lowered himself into one of the plush recliners across from the sofa.

"Gemma tells me about all the work you're doing to help her." He glanced toward the kitchen and lowered his voice. "She's a stubborn one." He gave a sad shake of his head. "Won't let us help her out at all."

"She wants to be independent and it's important for her to prove she can do things on her own," Cole responded. But as he thought more about that, his heart grew a little heavy. Gemma had a family who cared about her, and her cause, and wanted to help in the ways they knew how. How was that any different than what he was doing? Sure, her mother might want her to settle down because she worried about her safety, but that was natural maternal instinct. It didn't mean they didn't see her as a grown up, and weren't proud of her work. In fact, Gemma might be the only one who didn't understand that by continually pushing them away, she was coming across as narrow minded and maybe just a little bit young and selfish. Then again, who was he to call anyone selfish...?

"It's also important to know it's okay to ask family for help," Frank said. "Just like you know you can come to us too, right, Cole?" Cole caught the worry in Frank's eyes. Worry for him— the boy who'd practically grown up without a family, at least one who gave a shit about him. Cole grew a little more agitated that Gemma didn't see them for what they were. Frank and

Audrey were good people, treating him like a son and giving him more than a place to stay when he was a kid.

"Hey, are you two talking about me?" Gemma teased. She plunked herself down next to her father and he wrapped his arm around her.

He smiled at her and dropped a loving kiss onto her forehead. "Gemma, you might be a grown woman, but you'll always be my little girl and I'll always want to help you. Someday when you have kids of your own, you'll understand that."

Cole's heart hitched. The normalcy in all this reminded him of how much he wanted a family of his own, and how much he wanted it with Gemma.

Audrey came from the kitchen. "Dinner time." She smiled at Cole and proceeded to tell him about all the dishes she'd made for him. But when he got up from the recliner and spotted a table full of pictures, his appetite retreated like a band of soldiers caught in the crossfire.

He scanned the photos, stopping to examine the one of him and Brandon when they were fourteen and playing their favorite video game. Christ, the two of them had spent hours in front of the TV, until Audrey kicked them outdoors to get some fresh air. Brandon was a whiz with gaming and computers, and Cole always thought his friend should have gone to college instead of enlisting. His glance moved on to the picture of Brandon at his high school graduation, then to the one of Brandon looking like a proud soldier after graduating from basic training.

His heart tumbled in his chest and he fought the prick of tears as the memories shook him. Fuck, he missed him so much. When his hand tightened around his drink glass Gemma came up beside him. He couldn't help but flinch when she brushed her knuckles along his.

"You okay?"

"Yeah."

Turning from her, he followed Audrey to the dining room, which had been beautifully set for four. He sat and took another swig of his rum, praying it would wash down the emotions rising up in him.

After the meal was served, they talked mainly about Gemma's cause and how his speech had the benefactors opening their wallets. Cole was having a hard time concentrating on anything. Being back here with Brandon's family had him feeling raw and exposed, making it harder and harder for him to keep his shit together. And Cole always kept his shit together. Falling apart was not an option. Every now and then Gemma would cast a glance his way, worry moving over her eyes.

Soon anger moved into his stomach, because Audrey turned the conversation to Gemma and her marital status.

"Gemma, you rushed away so fast last night, I didn't get a chance to introduce you to Marie Johnson's son. He's a fine young boy."

Gemma cast Cole a glance and he got the distinct impression she wanted him to say something. But how could he come right out and tell Audrey and Frank what the two of them were doing behind closed doors?

Sadness moved over Gemma's face as she turned back to her mother. "Maybe next time," she said, and Cole fisted his hands, hating himself.

As Audrey continued to list off a bevy of bachelors who'd love to go out with her, pushing Gemma harder and harder, all Cole wanted to do was push back. He clenched down on his teeth in an effort to stop himself from telling everyone around the table how he really felt. Except he couldn't give Gemma what she wanted, and he wasn't the man her parents wanted for her.

Cole forced himself to eat, and once they finished their meal and the dishes were cleared, Audrey and Frank disappeared into the kitchen to make tea, leaving him alone with Gemma.

Blue eyes full of concern blinked up at him and he knew he needed to escape, to remove himself from all things that reminded him of Brandon, all things that reminded him he wasn't the guy for Gems.

"Want to go into the other room?" she asked quietly.

Cole pushed out of his chair and followed Gemma into the living room. Once again he was bombarded with pictures of his fallen friend.

"Are you okay, Cole?"

He glanced at the picture of Brandon in his formal military garb and his stomach twisted so hard he feared he was going to vomit. "He wasn't cut out for the army," he murmured under his breath.

"Don't you ever say that."

Cole's head came up with a start, surprised by the anger in her tone. "What?"

Fire lit Gemma's eyes as her hand went to the back of her neck. "Don't you ever say that about Brandon."

"What are you talking about? What's gotten into you?"

She rubbed the back of her neck furiously, her blue eyes flashing. "Brandon was a great soldier and a great man. Don't you ever say he wasn't."

Cole shook his head, his emotions in turmoil. "That's not what I meant."

"Then what did you mean?"

He exhaled slowly and took a moment to choose his words carefully. "He joined the army because of me. If he didn't follow in my footsteps, he'd be alive today."

"No, Cole. Brandon joined the army because he wanted to. His choices were his own. Don't you dare take responsibility for his actions. They were his and his alone."

She turned from him to glance at a childhood picture of a young Brandon and Gemma, brother and sister sitting on their horses eating ice cream. Cole stepped up to her and removed her hand from her neck. She leaned forward, her hair spilling over her shoulders and he worked to rub the tension from her muscles.

"I didn't mean..." he began, but his words died an abrupt death when he spotted the small tattoo at the base of her hairline. Hands shaking, he parted her curls, and his stomach recoiled when he saw the word *honor*.

"Gemma, what...when?"

She turned to face him and tilted her chin until their eyes met. "After Brandon died," she whispered.

Cole's voice was as shaky as his hands when he asked, "Is that why you always rub the back of your neck when someone mentions his name?"

She nodded. "Brandon was the most honorable man I knew, and this tattoo helps me remember him, but it also helps me let go. Know what I mean?"

Feeling like he'd been sucker punched, Cole faltered backward. Honor. That one word, and the meaning behind it had chaos erupting inside him, reminding him he'd failed the one man he owed everything to. He gripped his dog tags and squeezed until they cut skin. "I need to go." He swallowed the knot clogging his throat. "I really, really need to go."

She outstretched her arm but he flinched to avoid her touch. Confusion moved over her eyes as she snatched her hand back like it had been burned. Her gaze moved over his face and in a moment of desperation she said, "Cole, wait."

"No." He shook his head hard and after a quick consultation with himself he said, "This thing between us...it's wrong. What we've been doing is wrong." He pressed his palm to his forehead and fisted his hair. "So goddamn wrong."

"You don't mean that."

"Yes I do. I'm sorry I ever touched you." He backed up a few more inches and hardened himself when confusion turned to anger in her eyes. He was being a prick, of that he was certain, but he needed to get away from her. He needed her to see he wasn't sweet, and she deserved someone who would honor her brother, not dishonor him and everyone else the way he had.

"How can you say that?"

"I should have walked away from you that first night at the benefit. Just like I did that day you tried to seduce me in the barn."

"Cole." Tears pooled in her eyes and she wrapped her arms around herself, his words penetrating deeper than nuclear weaponry.

"Tell your folks I'm sorry, but I need to go."

Hurt registered in her eyes and he hated himself for putting it there—again—but he needed to get out of there, needed to be as far away from her as possible.

"Good-bye, Gemma."

Chapter Ten

Cole was in a bad mood. A kick-ass, shitty, stay-out-of-my-way kind of mood by the time he pulled his truck into the base. Dust kicked up under his tires as he came to a fast stop and slammed his vehicle into park. He climbed from the cab and shut his door with much more force than necessary before closing the gate behind him. All eyes turned to him but he ignored his comrades, who were already hard at work training their dogs.

Exhausted from a night of no sleep, he stomped toward the hangar. As if sensing his distress, Ralph came sauntering over to him.

"Hey, boy." Not wanting to upset the dog more than he already was, he bent, gave Ralph a good scrub behind the ears and said, "Come on. Let's go have some fun."

At least working with Ralph gave him something to think about other than how much he hated himself right now, not to mention the hurt he'd put in Gemma's eyes last night.

He took the dog inside the hangar. The two spent the rest of the morning going over drills, until Ralph headed off to his empty water bowl. Needing to refill it, Cole made his way to his truck to grab a jug. He walked past Jack without speaking, even though his friend was glaring at him with careful regard, like he knew how much of a fuckup Cole really was.

"You want to talk about it?" Jack asked as Cole offered his friend his back.

"No," he answered without stopping.

Cole grabbed the jug of water from his cooler and made his way back inside. When he reached the hangar, Ralph was nowhere to be found.

He left the hangar and shaded the morning sun from his eyes as he walked around the building and scanned the vast grounds surrounding the abandoned base. He whistled. "Hey, boy, where are you?" That's when he heard Ralph barking from the other side of the fence. Shit.

Jack came over to him and tossed a tennis ball from one hand to the other. "How did he get out there?"

Cole drove his hands into his pockets, and inspected the chain link fence. "He must have found a hole. He can be pretty damn wily."

As Ralph continued to bark, Jack scrubbed his chin and said, "Yeah, well right now he's pretty damn agitated about something."

"I'll go get him."

At the back of the compound, Cole walked along the fence until he found the small opening Ralph had used to escape. Cole pulled back the chain and crawled through, trying not to snag his fatigues in the process. He walked the empty field fringing the base, his boots pounding on the dry soil as he followed the howling sounds echoing in the air. As the barking grew louder, more frenzied, Cole hurried his steps. What was going on?

When Ralph let out a long whine, Cole took off running. He could hear the thundering of Jack's boots as he followed from behind.

"Hey, boy." Cole scanned the grounds and looked for possible threats as he closed the distance between them. "What's got you so riled up?" That's when he noticed all the debris on the ground. Cole slowed his steps, stepping over old cartridges, casings and scrap metal, some with deadly sharp edges.

As he took in the situation unfolding before him, he couldn't help but smile. Instead of digging at the scraps, Ralph was doing exactly what he was supposed to be doing. He'd found ammunition wreckage and was barking to warn his handler of danger.

"Well, I'll be damned. Way to go, boy."

As he approached the dog, Ralph turned his way and started running toward him, his big claws digging into the dry ground and creating a cloud of dust around them. Before Cole even realized what was happening, Ralph jumped on him and sent him flying backward.

"Whoa," Cole yelled out. He grabbed the dog by the scruff and tried to find his balance as he faltered.

Beefy paws took him to the ground and pain sliced along his legs as something sharp tore into his flesh. He hit the ground with a resounding thud, his head coming into contact with a hard, unforgiving object. He cringed, the sky coming in and out of focus, Ralph's bark a distant buzz. As the world faded away, his life flashed before his eyes and the last thing he remembered before everything went black, was Jack standing over him calling the others for help.

A long time later Cole blinked his eyes open and winced. Pain radiated from the top of his head all the way down to the base of his neck as the world swayed before him. Having no idea why his head was throbbing so damn bad, his hand went to the back of his skull to discover a peach-sized lump that hurt like a son of a bitch.

"Looks like he's going to live after all."

"What the hell?" Cole asked, blinking rapidly until the vision of Jack standing over him came into focus. Except Cole was no longer flat out on the ground, he quickly realized. He was in a strange bed, in a room that wasn't his own. "Where the hell am I?"

"The hospital."

"What happened?"

"Ralph happened."

Cole searched his mind. As he sorted through the chaos, the pieces slowly fell into place. "He was trying to protect me."

"Which isn't a bad thing," Jack said. "We just have to teach him another way of going about it. At least he took you down, instead of digging at the debris. You've made great progress with him. Gemma will be thrilled."

At the mention of Gemma, Cole's gut clenched and he tossed his blanket off. He made a move to get up but the room started spinning once again. His stomach turned upside down, and he stilled himself, gripping the mattress and striving not to vomit. "I need to get out of here."

"Easy, Cole, you've got a concussion." He gestured toward his leg. "As well as a nice gash on your calf."

"I hate hospitals."

"The doc said they could discharge you once you came to, but you can't stay alone tonight."

Cole closed his eyes, sleep pulling at him again as he thought about going home to an empty condo. Bile pushed into his throat, and he coughed. "I've got Charlie."

"You've got more than Charlie. Come on."

Jack helped him to his feet and into his clothes before he left to get the nurse. A short while later the doc came back to check on him. He gave instructions on how to care for his leg before signing the discharge papers and insisted, for precautionary measures, Cole needed to be under watch for the next twenty-four hours.

Cole climbed into the passenger seat of his truck and Jack drove him home. He immediately went to his bed and spent the rest of the day drifting in and out of sleep. He dreamed of Gemma. Gemma sitting with him, tucking him in, tending to his leg and dropping soft, loving kisses onto his forehead.

He also dreamed of Brandon. His friend. His fallen comrade. A man he'd failed.

The night seemed to go on forever. At least the pain in his head seemed to be lessening as the hours ticked by. By the time he was finally able to pull his eyes open and keep them open for any length of time, warm morning sunlight was shining in through the crack in his curtain.

A movement at the foot of the bed caught his attention, and he turned, expecting to see Jack watching over him. But what he saw instead had his pulse leaping and his mind racing a million miles an hour.

Gorgeous blue eyes full of tender concern met his. "Hey," was all Gemma said as she placed a clean bandage over his leg. She taped it down before she covered it back over with his blanket.

He swallowed the dryness in his throat as his pulse pounded at the base of his neck. "Gemma," he croaked out. His glance moved around the room, which had finally stopped spinning. He frowned, his dreams coming back to him. "I thought I was dreaming, but you've been here with me all night, haven't you?"

She came around his side of the bed, and handed him a glass of water. He only managed to swallow a few sips before his throat closed. She took it back, set it aside and turned her attention to the cloth soaking in a basin on his nightstand. She wrung it out and dabbed his forehead.

"Jack called me," she explained. Her concerned gaze panned his face and her voice whispered over him like a caress when she asked, "Are you feeling better?"

He briefly closed his eyes, love rushing to his heart as she tended to him. "Why did you come?"

Her hand fell away from his forehead and she looked at him as if he were dense. "Because you needed me."

With slow, careful movements, Cole propped himself up on his elbows. He shimmied backward until he was braced against his headboard. "Gemma, after I...what I said...I don't..." His voice trailed off as he looked at the woman he loved. Christ, after everything he did and the cruel things he'd said, he couldn't believe she was here, sitting by his side and taking care of him all night. She was an amazing woman, the most amazing woman he'd ever met, and he didn't deserve her compassion. He didn't deserve her.

A movement at the door had Gemma turning. "Jack," she said. "I'm glad you're here. Can you sit with him for a moment? I need to run to the clinic to take care of a couple of things. I also need to cancel my appointments for the day."

Cole reached out and grabbed her hand. She turned to him to meet his gaze directly, her blue eyes portraying her every emotion. "You don't have to do that," he said.

She took her hand from his and placed his arm by his side. When she leaned forward, her rich, sensual scent seeped under his skin and wrapped around his heart. He curled his fingers into fists and fought the urge to haul her into bed with him, to kiss away all the pain he'd inflicted on her, all the cruel words he'd aimed her way.

"You have no idea how much I do have to do that. But you will soon," she said. She walked away and paused at the door. "I'll bring back breakfast. Your fridge is empty."

Having no idea what she meant, he watched her go, then turned his attention to Jack as he lowered himself into the kitchen chair that had been brought into his bedroom.

"Did anyone ever tell you that you talk in your sleep?"

"Yeah, Brandon."

"Speaking of Brandon, you did a lot of talking to him last night. A lot of apologizing, actually."

Cole cringed and stared at the ceiling, wondering how much Gemma had heard of his unconscious ramblings.

Jack reached into his back pocket and pulled out Gemma's panties, the ones he'd stuffed in his glove box after fucking her that first night at the banquet. He twirled them around his finger and said, "I'm assuming all that apologizing has something to do with this."

Cole snatched the panties from his hand. "Fuck, Jack. What the hell do you think you're doing?"

Jack scoffed, "You were bleeding from the head, Cole, and I was looking for a first-aid kit or something to help stop the flow on the drive to the hospital. I found these in your glove box instead."

"You could have left them."

He gave an unapologetic shrug. "I could have, but I didn't."

Cole tucked the panties under his leg and stiffened as every memory of Gemma came rushing back. Jesus, what the hell had he gone and gotten himself into? He was well past the point of denying that things between them were casual or that he wasn't in love with her.

Jack gave a shake of his head, his eyes dark, questioning. "Cole, what the hell do you think you're doing?"

"It's none of your fucking business, Jack."

"You bet your ass it is. She's Brandon's sister and we're a brotherhood, which means it's all our business. Garrett's, Josh's and mine. If any of us are going to fuck around with a sibling of a fallen comrade, we should at least know what we're doing, don't you think?"

Everything in the way he'd so poetically phrased Cole's indiscretions had his stomach turning. Brandon didn't deserve this from him and Gemma didn't deserve the way he'd treated her the other night either. She was sweet, kind, loving and loyal, and had willingly opened herself to him. Handing herself over to him and trusting him implicitly while he was dishonoring everyone around him.

Cole fisted the bed sheets. "I love her, Jack."

Jack smiled and smacked him on the shoulder. "Well, now, there you go. It looks like you do know what you're doing, after all." He pushed back in his chair. "And it's about fucking time you realized it."

Confused by his reactions, Cole said, "What, you're not pissed because instead of taking care of Brandon's kid sister, I've been disloyal and sleeping with her?"

"Is that all you think you've been doing?" Jack inquired with one raised eyebrow.

Cole exhaled slowly, his head hurting, but not from the accident. He exchanged a look with his friend and wondered where this conversation was going. "What are you getting at?"

"You haven't been sleeping with her, pal. You've been falling for her. Hell, I think you've always loved her anyway. You have this twisted sense of loyalty to Brandon."

"Twisted? I owe that man so much, Jack. You have no idea."

"Cole, did you ever stop to think maybe on some level Brandon knew you always loved Gemma and maybe this was his way of driving you two together?"

Cole went quiet for a moment, then angled his head. "Have you been taking shrink classes, pal?"

Jack laughed and toyed with his dog tags. "No, but I've been to enough of them to know how this all works." He got quiet for a moment, like he was thinking about his own demons, before saying, "I know Brandon asked you to watch over her, but she's a strong, independent woman. Maybe she's not in need of your protection."

Cole went quiet and considered the last month he'd spent with her and how she made him feel something other than loss and sadness. He'd thought about how much he loved having her in his life, how strong and independent she was and how he loved the normalcy of sitting down to a meal after a workday. He loved how they laughed and how they shared the good days and the bad.

His mind went back to the time at her clinic, to when that little girl was there picking out a puppy with her parents. Cole's heart hitched, because he wanted a family like that of his own. And he wanted it with Gemma.

If Brandon could see her now, he'd see how self-sufficient and courageous she was. He'd see the amazing woman she'd turned out to be, a woman who'd stayed by Cole's side when he needed her and was not only capable of taking care of herself, but was capable of taking care of him too. Brandon would be damn proud of the woman she'd become. And maybe, just maybe, Jack was right and she didn't need his protection. Maybe she only needed his love.

Cole buried his face in his hands and by small degrees his body tightened. "Oh fuck."

"What?"

"I totally screwed everything up."

Jack's bark of laughter echoed in the room. "Well, now, that wouldn't surprise me one little bit. But don't worry, pal. Gemma came when I called her, so she might not hate you as much as you think."

Cole closed his eyes and muttered curses of frustration under his breath as his mind raced, trying to figure out what he could do or say to make it right between them. "I need to figure out a way to fix this."

Chapter Eleven

Armed with hot coffee and breakfast burritos from her favorite café, Gemma made her way back to Cole's condo. She'd learned so much about the tortured soldier when he fled from her parents' apartment two nights ago. Even more last evening when he'd laid there in his bed mumbling in his sleep. He'd unconsciously reached out to her as he fought his innermost demons. As she held him in her arms it had become glaringly apparent he'd never gotten over the loss of his best friend, never learned to let go.

Cole was the toughest guy she knew and instead of grieving after Brandon's death, he kept soldiering on. He'd buried his feelings behind some protective barrier that needed to come tumbling down before those destructive emotions ate him up inside. Deep in her heart Gemma knew Cole loved her, of that she was certain, but there was no way he could go forward until he learned to let go of the past. And she was just the girl to help him.

Armed with a plan, she climbed his stairs, but when she reached his front door and was about to twist the knob the door flung open and she found herself standing face to face with Cole.

Dark, tormented eyes met hers. "Gemma," he murmured.

Worry moved into her stomach as she took in his pallor. "Should you be up so soon?"

He touched the back of his head. "I'm okay. The swelling is down." He paused for a second and his voice dropped an octave when he said, "We need to talk."

Gemma exhaled slowly. "I know."

"About the other night," he began, getting right to the point. "I never meant—"

"Yes, you did," she said, cutting him off. "At the time, when you said you were sorry you ever touched me, you meant every word of it."

Deep sadness moved over his face and he fisted his hair. "I fucked this up, didn't I?"

She held up the brown paper bag and a tray holding two cups of coffee. "Do you think we can eat these in the car?"

He gave her a perplexed frown and rolled one shoulder. "I guess. If you want to."

"I want to take you somewhere."

"Where?"

Instead of telling him, for fear he might flat out refuse, she turned from him. "Come on."

Favoring his sore leg, Cole followed her down the steps and across the street. Once he was seated next to her in the car, she handed him his coffee and burrito.

He dug into his food like a man starved, and Gemma flicked on the radio before digging into her own. She maneuvered through city traffic, then shot Cole a glance as she pulled onto the highway. She drove for a long time and silence hung heavy, until she pulled off on the exit leading to her childhood ranch.

Cole frowned, and shifted uncomfortably in the seat beside her. "Where are you taking me?"

"Somewhere I should have taken you a long time ago. But I'd been so caught up in my own needs, I hadn't stopped to consider yours."

"What are you talking about?"

Instead of answering, Gemma pulled her car into the long, winding driveway leading to the ranch. She felt tension move through his body.

His jaw clenched and his shoulders stiffened. "I don't want to be here."

She turned to face him, and touched his arm. "I know you don't, but will you do this for me?"

He scrubbed his face. "That's hitting low, because you know I'd do anything for you."

"And I'd do anything for you, which is why you need to come with me." She parked her car and climbed from the seat. Fishing her old house key from her purse, she made her way to the front door. Cole sat in the car for a second longer and she wondered if he'd come. But then he opened his door and met her on the stairs.

He looked at his feet. "I don't think—"

"I do. Come on," she said. "No one is here but us. My folks are still in the city."

She pushed the door open and grabbed his hand before he could escape. Once inside the empty house, she immediately led Cole to Brandon's room. It had been redone since he'd lived here, but the essence of Brandon was still alive and impregnated in every object.

Cole sucked in a sharp breath and gripped his dog tags. "Why are you doing this?"

"Come sit." She led him to the bed. When he sank into the cushy mattress, she perched beside him and shimmied close, offering her support because he was going to need it. "I want to talk about Brandon." She grabbed the photo album off the bookshelf and the smell of old paper hit her when she peeled it open.

She pointed to one of the photos and smiled up at Cole. "Remember this day?"

Cole narrowed his eyes as he looked at the picture of him and Brandon riding a roller coaster when the fair had come to town. "What I remember about that day is you eating too much junk food and getting sick," he said.

She pulled a face. "Yeah, I still can't eat cotton candy to this day. How about these?" She redirected his attention as she flipped through the pages, showing him pictures of Brandon and Cole through the years. They spent a long time looking through the album, and when they came to the end she pointed to the picture of Cole and Brandon fishing, a small smile tugged at Cole's mouth.

"You like this one?" she asked.

"What I remember about that day is Brandon chasing you with a fish and you running home screaming bloody murder."

She cut him a sharp glance. "That was gross, Cole."

Cole laughed. "He sure caught shit that day."

"Yeah, well, he never got into that much trouble. Not when he always had you backing him up."

As soon as the words left her mouth, his smile dissolved and raw emotions passed over his eyes. He pressed his palms to his forehead. "Oh, Jesus, Gemma. Jesus. Jesus. Jesus."

He slipped off the mattress and sank to his knees. She could hear his breathing change, see his body begin to shake.

Gemma climbed from the bed and stood before him. She ran soothing fingers though his hair.

"It's okay, Cole. Let it out," she said, knowing how hard it was for him to allow himself to come undone. "Sometimes we have to fall apart before we can begin to put the pieces together again."

He reached out to her and pulled her to him, his hands wrapping around her waist as he buried his face in her stomach.

His breath was hot on her skin and she could feel his heart thundering. "I miss him so fucking much," he said, his voice rough with emotion.

Tears filled Gemma's eyes. "I know you do. We all do."

"He saved me, Gemma. When I was a kid, my father was a cruel bastard. Brandon gave me a place to stay and a family to love. Don't you see, he saved me?"

She dropped to her knees in front of him and cupped his cheeks. "You saved him too. He was a shy kid, and when you came into his life it saved him in so many ways."

Cole's breath came quicker as he brushed his thumb over her tears. "He asked me to take care of you, Gemma, and I thought I failed him—"

"You didn't fail him." Her gaze moved over his face. "If my brother treasured you enough to put me in your hands, don't you think he treasured you enough to let you put me in your heart too?"

Cole blinked and she saw love shining in his eyes when they met hers. Her heart flipped in her chest, everything inside her reaching out to him. "I know," he said. "I came to terms with that earlier today."

Her breath caught. "You did?"

"Yeah, when you showed up at my door, I was on my way to find you to tell you how much I loved you and how much I wanted to be with you. But then I thought I'd lost you. I couldn't take losing you too, Gems."

"You didn't lose me." Her stomach soared with joy and more tears fell. "But before we can build a future together you have to come to terms with Brandon's death and learn to let go." She touched the back of her neck. "Healing takes time, and you've never given yourself that."

He rested his elbows on his knees and shook his head. "I don't want to forget."

"Letting go isn't the same as forgetting. My tattoo is a symbol of comfort. It helps me remember, but it also helps me let go of the pain of loss."

She grabbed his dog tags and placed them in his hands. "That's what these are going to do for you. When you hold them, I want you to remember Brandon, but then I want you to exhale and when you breathe out, let the pain of loss go with it. It's what he would have wanted."

After a long moment of silence, Cole exhaled slowly, and she could almost feel the wall he'd built around his heart come tumbling down.

"He was a great man and a great soldier."

"Yes, he was." She breathed out slowly and said, "And I bet he's looking down at you right now and calling you a dumbass for the way you've been acting."

He grinned but his voice was shaky when he said, "When did you get so damn smart?"

With Cole finally opening himself up to her, reaching out to her emotionally, she said, "When you were off fighting a war and I was home waiting for you to come back to me."

He nodded, like he understood. "I guess we have a lot of time to make up for."

Gemma's thoughts went back to the day she seduced him in the barn. "Ten years to be exact."

He shook his head, and for the umpteenth time, went on to explain, "Jesus, Gemma, you were a kid."

"And I'm not anymore."

He drew her to him and held her for a long time, and she could feel his shoulders relax, the weight of the world no longer bearing down on them. They stayed together like that for a long, long time. Gemma remained silent, letting Cole come to terms with what he needed to do. The time ticked by and she listened to his breathing settle and his heart rate return to normal.

Cole finally broke the quiet and asked, "What did I ever do to get so lucky to have you in my life?"

"Well I could stay here and list off all the times you came to my rescue when we were younger, or..." She let her voice trail off, stood and reached for him.

"Or what?"

"Come with me."

Cole stood. "Where are you taking me now?"

They exited the house and Gemma led him to the barn at the back of the homestead. She pulled open the doors and the scent of hay filled her senses, bringing her back to her childhood.

She waved toward the hay pile. "I want you to make love to me. Here, where I always wanted our first time to be."

A pained look came over his face and he faltered backward. "No, Gems. This is wrong."

The air around them grew heavy with the scent of their arousal when his mouth took full possession of her sex. He ran the soft blade of his tongue all the way from the bottom to the top and spent a few extra minutes on her clit as he dipped a finger inside her. Stroking her deep, he prepared her for his girth.

Her senses exploded, pleasure swamping her. She began moving her hips. "Cole," she murmured, loving how his name sounded on her tongue as he pleasured her and knowing it would be the last man's name she'd ever call out during lovemaking.

"Gemma," he murmured as he climbed up her body.

She wrapped her arms around him and held tight when he entered her. They began moving together, each giving and taking, and this time their lovemaking was less rushed, less frenzied, as Cole reintroduced himself to her body. Not as a casual lover this time, but as a committed partner who'd be there for the good times and the bad. Even though their movements were less hurried, and he touched her with slow hands, the way they were coming together was every bit as powerful and potent as their first time. Their orgasms came at the same time, and afterward they stayed together, neither wanting to be the first to move.

A long time later Cole rolled off her and gathered her into his arms. He turned to her and brushed his thumb over her well-kissed lips. He looked thoughtful, contemplative, as he looked at her.

"What?" she asked.

"You're a beautiful, independent woman, Gemma, and after all we've been through I understand you're not in need of my protection, you're only in need of my love."

She smiled up at him. "I might be quite capable of taking care of myself, but I kind of like it when you can take care of me. You showed me that it's okay to ask for help when you need it and accept it when it's offered."

He gave her a sheepish look. "Well, I kind of like it when you take care of me too."

She laughed, knowing he was talking about the night at the hotel in Dallas. She gave him a playful whack and said, "I bet you do."

"Just so you know, Gemma, it was never just sex with you." He brushed her hair off her face. "Do you remember when you once asked me what I wanted?"

"Yes, and you told me...no wars, no death, no more loss."

"I wasn't entirely truthful, because I left your name off that list. None of those things are important without you in my life. I want you to marry me, Gemma. I want you to be my wife."

Cloaked in contentment, she pressed her lips to his. His kiss was full of tenderness and emotion as he held her tight, waiting for her answer. "And I want you to be my husband, Cole. I always have."

Their lips met once again and they shared an intimate kiss. Cole inched back and the emotions on his face nearly stopped her heart. "Do you think someday, maybe someday soon, you might think about coming off the pill?"

"I'll never take it again," she said, thrilled to know he wanted to have a family with her.

A crooked smile turned up the corners of his mouth and his eyes were teasing when he gripped her hips. "It's a good thing you've got these wide birthing hips, because I want a huge family."

Feigning insult, Gemma smacked him hard. "Hey, I do not have wide birthing hips!"

When his laugh died down he grimaced and asked, "How do you think your mother is going to take this?"

Gemma smiled. "Believe me, she's going to be thrilled."

"Thrilled? I hardly think so. I was sitting next to her at the banquet when she invited that guy over. Jesus, it was all I could do to keep it together as I listened to her try to marry you off."

"So that's what the commotion was all about." She shook her head, a small smile on her mouth. "I figured it was something like that."

"Yeah, so let me tell you, she's not going to be thrilled. I'm hardly a rich benef—"

She pressed her finger to his lips. "After you ran out of her house, she insisted I go after you. That's when I realized what she's been up to, aggressively trying to marry me off since you got back home."

"You lost me, Gems."

"She knew all along how we felt about each other and was pushing our buttons. She's very good at pushing buttons and getting what she wants."

He wagged his finger back and forth between the two of them. "You mean she wanted...?"

Gemma nodded.

He shook his head. "Jesus, I had no idea."

"Neither did I until I saw the look on her face after you stormed out of her place." She snuggled in close. "She's going to be so happy." She lowered her voice before adding, "So is Brandon. I know he's looking down at us with a big smile on his face."

At the mention of his fallen friend, Cole gripped his dog tags. He breathed deep and let it out slowly, his face relaxing as he let go the pain of loss.

A second later, he cupped her chin, his eyes serious. "Maybe it's time for you to let go of a few things too."

Gemma nodded, knowing full well what he was talking about and how foolish and childish she'd been by not asking for help when she needed it. Was proving her independence more important than her cause? And really, did any parent ever see their kids as grown up? Sadly enough, this whole time she'd been turning her family away when Cole had spent his whole life chasing one. It was a mistake she was about to rectify. "You're right. I should call my mother."

Cole gave her a smile that said how proud he was of her and jumped to his feet. He grabbed Gemma's hand and tugged. "Come on."

"Where?"

He gathered up their clothes. "Back to the city."

"Right now?" She tugged on her shirt and pants.

"Yes, right now." He dressed quickly, then said, "You need to call your mother, and I need to go tell the guys we're getting married."

"Do we have to do that right away?"

"Yes, I want the world to know, and then we need to go shopping. We're going to have to find you that house with the white picket fence if we're going to accommodate both of us, a horde of kids and three dogs."

"Three dogs?"

His mouth turned up at the corner, making him look so damn sexy, it had Gemma aching to rip off his clothes and sink back into the hay with him again. "Yeah, let's go get Nana."

Gemma's heart turned over in her chest and she went up on her toes to kiss him on the mouth. He lifted her clear off her feet and kissed her back.

When he finally let her go, Gemma touched his cheek. "So tough, so rough and so damn rugged," she whispered. "But still so sweet. So very, very sweet."

His Strings to Pull

Cathryn Fox

Dedication

To the team behind my series. Thank you all for helping me make these stories shine!

Chapter One

With a rescue tube tucked under her arm, lifeguard Jenny Andersen walked the length of the outdoor pool, keeping one eye on the kids splashing and playing in the shallow end and the other on the gorgeous man peeling his shirt off near the lounge chairs directly across from her. Two young girls ran around him, and with a playful look on his face, he twisted his towel and snapped them gently on their rear ends to shoo them away. As they squealed and jumped in the water, Jenny couldn't help but smile at his antics, nor could she help but wonder if those rambunctious kids were his. Her glance strayed to his left hand, but past experiences had taught her that a ring-free finger meant little or nothing.

He moved to the deep end of the pool, each stride of his long, muscled legs purposeful and sexy. He stretched his arms over his shaved head, and his tanned, athletic body glistened invitingly in the early morning sun. Jenny noted the way all the women were watching, or rather, drooling, from the comfort of their lounge chairs.

Speaking of drooling...

Her glance slid up the length of him to broad shoulders covered in tattoos, before traveling downward again. Good God, his body was like a Plinko game, all hard ridges and muscles that guided her gaze down to the jackpot hidden beneath a pair of low hanging swimming trunks. She swallowed against her suddenly dry throat and damn near died when she looked back to his face to find him watching her. He gave her a playful, lopsided grin that further weakened her already wobbly knees, and then dove into the water, leaving her wondering what the hell it was about him that left her panting like a sheep dog in the sweltering heat of the summer.

Watching his long frame glide through the rippling waves, she once again wondered if he was taken. But thinking about his marital status had her thoughts going back to her last relationship. She gave a disgruntled shake of her head, hardly able to believe that her ex had had a wife and kids waiting for him at home. Looking back, all the signs had been there—they could never go back to his place, the phone calls he had to leave the room to take, the nights he said he was out of town on business and couldn't call her—she'd just been too blinded by infatuation, too trusting, to see them for what they were.

Honestly, didn't anyone believe in monogamy anymore? Were there no guys out there looking for the same thing as her? She wanted what her parents had before her dad died a few years ago—love, trust, respect. Was that so much to ask for?

Sadly, she was beginning to think so.

She watched the tattooed hottie surface in the shallow end. Like a fish drawn to a shiny lure, she walked the length of the pool toward him. The young girls he'd been snapping earlier jumped all over him, trying to drag him under the water. Jenny recognized the children he was with. Their townhouse was in walking distance of the community pool, and they came here often with their mother. Jenny had never seen them with this man before, however. Perhaps, like her brother, Garrett, he was a military man, and had recently returned home from overseas.

He picked one of the girls up and tossed her into the water. Jenny stopped abruptly, drawn to the fun-loving scene, but as her feet came to a sudden halt, something, or someone, crashed into her from behind. Before she even realized what was happening, the rescue tube flew out of her hand and she landed in the water with an undignified belly flop.

Her hands flailed, and as she gasped for air and worked to find her footing, a strong pair of arms lifted her from the water. She opened her mouth and closed it again, struggling to fill her deflated lungs. Not because she'd taken in water, but because the tattooed hottie was looking down at her with dark eyes she could so easily lose herself in.

She opened her mouth to tell him she was okay, but no sound came. She blinked rapidly, trying to clear her lust-filled brain as she struggled to take in air.

"Shit," he said. The next thing she knew she was flat on her back on the flagstone walkway surrounding the pool, and Mr. Hottie's lips were coming down fast.

Oh, God, his mouth tasted like cool mint and warm cinnamon all rolled into one. His lips moved over hers, and as air filled her lungs in a whoosh, she was sure she'd just drowned and gone to heaven. And oh, what a heaven it was...

As though moving on their own accord, her arms tangled around his neck, holding his mouth to hers as she reveled in his warmth, the sweet flavor of his kisses. She searched for his tongue, wanting a deeper, more thorough taste, but before she could find it, his body stiffened and he inched back.

He angled his head, and when eyes full of concern locked on hers, reality crashed over her like a cold wave. Oh hell. He was performing CPR, not kissing her.

"I...uh..." she managed to get out, then for good measure, she sucked in a breath and coughed to make it look like she *was* having a near-death experience, but the look on his face told her he was on to her.

He swiped his tongue over his lower lip, like he was savoring the taste of her, as he eyed her curiously. "Wait...you weren't...were you..." he began, his body still hovering over hers, his mouth so close all she had to do was lift herself up an inch if she wanted to steal another kiss.

Which, of course, she did...

"Yes, I was drowning," she said quickly. "But thanks to your quick thinking, I'm okay now." When she saw the other lifeguard coming her way, she held her hand up to stop her, letting her know she was fine. She made a move to get up, but he leaned in, keeping her pinned with his hard body. Her mind took that moment to wander, wondering what it would be like to be sandwiched between this man—and a mattress—their bodies naked, entwined...

"Hey, lady, you okay?"

The sound of a kid's voice put an abrupt end to her fantasy. She turned her head to see a boy around twelve hovering over her, and instantly recognized him as the big brother to the two young girls this man had been playing with earlier.

"I'm sorry." The boy crinkled his nose apologetically. "I didn't see you."

"You're not supposed to be running on the deck," Jenny said firmly, surprised she could actually find her voice as the man's weight continued to press down on her.

Mr. Hottie swung his head toward the boy. "We'll discuss this later, when we get home," he said, his expression stern yet affectionate at the same time.

They'd discuss it at home? Jenny's heart sank. Damn, the kids *were* his, which meant he was likely married to the pretty woman who brought them here often.

She tried to move, shoving at his chest, but it was like trying to push a pickup with a toothpick. "If you'll excuse me..." she began.

"Ving."

"What?" she asked.

"It's Ving," he said. "Ving Duncan."

"Okay, Ving Duncan." She gave another hard shove, needing him off her body before he noticed the hardening of her nipples beneath her speedo. Cripes, the guy was married and the last thing she wanted to do was lust after someone's husband again. "If you could just move."

He jumped to his feet and pulled her up with him. Her body collided with his, and as his hardness meshed with her softness, it damn near sucked the oxygen from her lungs— again.

"And you are?" he asked.

"Grateful that you saved me. Thank you." Working to tamp down the heat he stirred in her, she turned to the boy, and put on her best serious face. "You need to be careful. You could have really hurt someone."

"I'm sorry," he said again, hanging his head, and Jenny, having a soft spot for kids, ruffled his hair. She shot Ving an imploring look, and said, "Don't be too hard on him. He seems like a nice kid, and I don't think he meant it."

"Maybe," he responded. "But that doesn't mean he's not going to get the whipper snapper." He reached for the nearest towel and began spinning it. The boy screeched and jumped into the water.

Jenny smiled and shook her head. Ving looked so tough and rugged, but underneath all that tattooed hardness it was easy to tell he was a softie at heart. "You're a good dad."

"I'm not—" Before he could finish his youngest girl came along and snapped him with her towel. He yelped and turned. "Hey," he said, taking off after her as she shrieked and chuckled loudly.

"No running," Jenny called out, and as they slowed to a fast walk, Ving tossed a sheepish smirk her way. Jenny wagged her finger. "Or you'll all be getting *my* whipper snapper."

Something that looked like intrigue moved over his face, and his grin turned playful when he turned back to her. He arched one brow and said, "When you put it that way, it makes me want to run all the more."

Jenny laughed and waved him off, not about to go there with him. She turned her attention to the kids playing in the deep end, all the while trying to calm her overexcited body and forget she ever met Ving Duncan.

God, why were all the good ones married?

"What the hell is the matter with you?" Garrett Andersen asked as he shaded the late afternoon sun from his eyes.

Ving stood inside the gates of the old abandoned base where his comrades were training service dogs, and snatched a tennis ball off the ground. He squeezed it in his palm, then tossed it. The shaggy dog he'd picked up earlier at the shelter— and decided to take under his wing—ran after it as he turned his attention to his buddy, Garrett.

"What?" Ving asked.

"Don't 'what' me. You've been walking around all afternoon with a stupid ass grin on your face."

Ving feigned innocence, even though he knew Garrett was right. He couldn't stop smiling since he left the pool earlier that morning. "I am?"

"Yeah, you are." Garrett's glance moved to Ving's shaved head, then his gaze dropped to the tattoos decorating Ving's shoulders. "Don't you think this whole village idiot thing is kind of contradictory to the image you're going for?" Garrett asked.

Ving laughed. "Why don't you tell me what you really think?"

"Why don't you tell me what's going on?"

When the dog came back, Ving took the ball from her mouth. "Good girl," he said, and as he tossed it again, his mind went back to the hot lifeguard he'd met earlier that day. She was so sweet, the kind of girl he could bring home to his mother. Christ, where the hell had that thought come from? He'd only just met her, and even though he didn't believe in love at first sight—lust maybe—he couldn't get her out of his thoughts.

She was good with Andy after he'd knocked her into the pool, and he didn't miss the way she kept smiling down at him when he was playing with Marley and Kate. Nor did he miss the way she was looking at him with those big sapphire-blue eyes he could drown in—eyes not at all unlike the ones glaring at him now.

"Ah, shit, it's a girl, isn't it?" Garrett asked.

"Yeah," he said, tenting his fingers like he always did when in deep thought.

Just then Luke Phillips, former army security specialist, stepped up to them and patted Ving on the shoulder. He took one look at Ving's face, furrowed his brows and said, "Okay, what's her name?"

The dog came back and Ving bent forward to give her a pat on her head. "I don't know. I thought I'd let the kids name her."

"You know that's not who I'm talking about," Luke said.

Ving straightened and decided not to make this too easy on them. "Then who are you talking about?"

"The girl who's got you all tied up in knots, that's who." Luke said. "Now stop fucking around and tell me who she is."

"What makes you think a girl's got me all tied up?"

"Because you can't stop smiling and you're walking around like a love-struck dumb ass," Garrett explained.

"So spill," Luke said. "Tell us her name."

"I would if I could."

"If you're going to fall in love with a girl, don't you think you should at least get her name first?" Luke asked.

"I might not know her name, but I kissed her." He grinned and added, "Well, technically it wasn't a kiss."

Garrett laughed. "Then what was it, technically?"

Ving scrubbed a hand over his head and gave them a crooked smile. "More like I performed mouth-to-mouth."

Luke scoffed, and shook his head. "Mouth-to-mouth?"

"I was at the pool with the kids and Andy bumped into the lifeguard," Ving explained. "She fell into the water and I thought she was drowning. So I performed mouth-to-mouth. Except she started kissing me, and well, I don't know, she was just so damn beautiful and nice, that I fell for her." He snapped his fingers. "Just like that." He looked skyward. "Oh, man, you should have seen her. Big blue eyes, long legs, the face of an angel. So sweet, so damn sweet. And funny too."

Garrett narrowed his eyes and Ving didn't miss the way his nostrils were flaring.

"What the hell is the matter with you?" Ving asked.

"What pool were you at?" Garrett growled.

"Glenmore Community Pool. Why?"

Luke took step back. "Oh shit. Sounds like he's talking about Jenny."

Ving turned to Luke. "You know her?"

"Yeah, I know her. So does Garrett." With a nod, he gestured toward Garrett, like there was something funny about all this. "He knows her really well, don't you, Garrett?"

Ah shit. That meant Jenny was Garrett's girl. Ving's heart sank because he and Garrett weren't just comrades, they were friends, and had spent many nights surviving together overseas. Even if Ving owed the man a proper beating for putting a snake in his sleeping bag—damn he hated snakes—no way in hell would he ever come between Garrett and his girl. No matter how much of an angel she was.

"She's your girl," Ving said, nodding in understanding as he kicked a rock across the compound.

"No, she's not my girl. She's my sister."

Ving's heart soared. "No way!"

Garrett fisted his hands and said, "Way."

"Sweet!"

Garrett widened his stance. "What's so sweet about it?"

"Now I can ask her out."

"Ving, come on, she's my kid sister and you're a..."

"I'm a what?"

Garrett scrubbed his chin and looked past Ving's shoulders like he was in deep thought. "You're a..."

When his words drifted off, Ving pressed, "What's the problem? You never had any trouble telling me what you thought before."

"That's because my sister wasn't involved."

"And you think I'll hurt her?" Garrett exhaled slowly, and when he went quiet, Ving added, "I think you know me better than that."

"You're right," Garrett said slowly. "I do."

Ving smiled, because Garrett *did* know better. Unlike most of their comrades who were looking for no strings, Ving wanted it all. When they were overseas, Ving always talked to Garrett about settling down and having kids. His friend knew he wasn't one to go home with a different girl every night, even though he had plenty of offers.

"But she's my sister!" Garrett said, running agitated hands through his hair.

"You know I'd never mess with a comrade's sister if I seriously didn't want to get to know her better." Ving held his hands out at his sides. "I mean come on. I have a sister too. If any one of you guys messed with Tally, well...let's just say there'd be hell to pay, and you all know why."

Garrett nodded and visibly relaxed. "Jenny's a nice kid and deserves a nice guy. If it was anyone but you, I'd be kicking some ass."

"Thanks, man," Ving said. "So you're cool with me going out with her?"

Garrett cocked his head. "You'll have to get her to say yes first."

"Yeah, and she's not one to fall for any stupid pick-up lines, either," Luke said. Both guys rounded on Luke. "What?" he asked, taking a small step back. When they continued to glare at him he lifted his hands, palms out. "All I'm saying is she's too smart to fall for the lines. If you want to get the attention of a beautiful and intelligent girl like her, you'll have to be a little more creative."

As Ving considered that and thought about how they met, a wicked idea formed in the back of his mind. Oh yeah, he knew just what he had to do to get her attention and coax a yes from her lips. And if things played out according to the half-cocked plan racing around his brain, he wouldn't just get a date, he'd get to feel that sweet mouth of hers on his again too.

Chapter Two

Jenny adjusted the strap on her bathing suit and strolled the length of the pool, reveling in the warmth of the morning sun shining down on her. As she watched a group of kids play in the shallow end, her thoughts drifted to her encounter with Ving yesterday.

Ving Duncan

Hot, hard, funny…*married.*

Even though she knew she should put him out of her mind, her glance kept straying to the row of townhouses down the road from the community center. Yes, despite knowing he was taken, after their run-in yesterday she'd still found herself watching him walk home with his three children in tow. A movement on the sidewalk drew her attention. She turned and when she spotted Ving and his little ones coming her way, her heart raced. She quickly put her back to them, forcing her attention on her pool duties.

Just then fellow lifeguard, Candace Simms, came up to her and nodded toward Ving. "Your hottie is back."

"*My* hottie?" Jenny asked, planting a hand on her hip in defense, even though she wished it was true. "He's not my anything."

Candace wagged her eyebrows. "Yeah, well, you didn't see the way he was looking at you yesterday."

Jenny's heart leapt and, while she wanted to hear all the details, wanted to gossip like a smitten high school girl, she said, "He's taken, Candace."

"Hmmmm," she said, sneaking looks at him.

"What?" Jenny asked, getting the sense that Candace knew something she didn't.

"Taken or not, he's still nice to look at."

"That he is," Jenny agreed, deciding to give her friend that much.

As she chatted with Candace about the new summer schedule, Jenny watched Ving jump into the water and roughhouse with his kids. Despite her best efforts not to pay him any attention, her glance kept straying his way. A few minutes later he swam out to the deep end, and when he began thrashing, merely a few feet from her, Candace grabbed Jenny's arm.

"Shit," she said. "He's in trouble."

Acting purely on instincts, both Candace and Jenny jumped into the pool. Working together they pulled him out. Within seconds they had him laid out on the pool deck.

"He needs mouth-to-mouth," Candace said as she checked his vitals. "Hurry, Jenny."

Trusting her friend's judgment, Jenny positioned his head and quickly pressed her mouth to his. But the second her lips closed over his, his hands circled around her back, pulling her on top of him.

Wait...is he...?

Coherent thought fled as he began to kiss her, and when she felt the rough pad of his thumb on the back of her neck, holding her tightly against him, lust prowled through her body.

Oh Gawd...

She burned as he devoured her with his mouth, need zinging through her veins at breakneck speed. His tongue slipped inside her mouth and tangled with hers, and her body responded with a shudder.

"Eww, Ving that's gross."

Jenny pulled back and drew in a fortifying breath when she found one of his little girls standing beside them. She looked back at Ving, who had a mischievous gleam in his eyes.

"What...what do you think you're doing?" she asked.

"What am I doing?" he retaliated. "It's more like what are you doing." He gestured with a nod toward the water. "I was just splashing around, and the next thing I knew you had me on the ground with your lips on mine."

"But I thought you were... Candace said..." When he gave her a lopsided grin, her words dissolved like honey in hot water. God, did he have to be so adorable. "But why would you...you're married."

He shook his head. "No I'm not."

She looked up to see his little girl staring at her. "You have kids."

"Kids? What are you talking about? I don't even like kids." He winked at the girl and she giggled and ran off. "Heck, I didn't even like myself when I was a kid."

"But I thought—"

"I'm the babysitter. Do you think they would they call me Ving if I was their dad?"

Jenny considered that for a moment. "I guess not."

"So I'm not married with kids, does that mean you'll go out with me now?"

"What?" she asked and looked around at all the people still staring at them. When she caught the way Candace was smirking at her, understanding dawned. She shook her head, incredulous; hardly able to believe that Candace was in on this. "You orchestrated this whole thing just to ask me out."

"And to kiss you."

Despite herself, Jenny laughed. Honestly, even though what he did was inappropriate and dangerous—and had taken her attention off the kids—she couldn't help but feel a bit flattered. No man had ever gone to such measures to get her attention before.

"I don't even know you," Jenny said.

"I've rescue kissed you, you've rescue kissed me. What more do you want to know?"

She narrowed her eyes and planted one hand on her hip. "How do I really know you're not married and these kids aren't yours?"

"Well, Jenny," he said. "You could always ask your brother, Garrett."

Her head came back with a start, not only because he knew her name but he also knew her brother. "Wait, you know Garrett?"

"Yeah, we served together."

"You did?"

He nodded. "And yesterday at the training compound, I told him I wanted to ask you out and he gave me his blessings."

"His blessings?" She laughed, and wondered if he came from a religious family. "Sounds like you were asking for my hand in marriage."

He arched a brow, and once again gifted her with that sexy grin that turned her knees to pudding. "All in good time, but first I have to prove to you how awesome I am."

195

"Pretty sure of yourself, aren't you?" When she shook her head, loving how funny and easy he was to be with, a wayward strand of hair fell forward. He reached out and tucked it behind her ear. Her entire body came alive at his touch. She looked deep into his eyes, noting the thoughtful way he looked at her. While most military men she knew were players, out with a different girl every night, Ving had a real kindness, a genuine honesty about him.

Then again, her track record had proved she was a terrible judge of character.

"So what do you say? Can I pick you up at seven?"

"No, you can't." When the smile fell from his face and he gave her a look that was so lost, so dejected, she said, "I work a split shift today and won't be ready until eight."

Ving drove around Jenny's neighborhood, one eye on the road, the other on the dashboard clock. Jesus, whoever said time was linear had no idea what they were talking about because tonight each minute felt more like ten.

He passed by her place again, but he was so goddamn excited to see her, he'd pulled into her driveway, despite being ten minutes early, and jammed his truck into Park. He grabbed the bouquet of flowers he'd picked up earlier and rushed up the long walkway leading to her condo.

He knocked and waited for a second. Just as he was about to knock again, the door flung open and he came face to face with a pretty blonde girl covered in tattoos and piercings.

"You must be Ving," she said, her gaze dropping to the flowers.

"I am, and you are?"

She crinkled her nose. "What kind of name is Ving anyway? Is it short for something?"

Before he could answer, Jenny came up behind her. "I see you met my nosey roommate, Samantha."

Samantha rolled her eyes. "It's Sam. She just calls me that to piss me off."

"Hi, Sam," Ving said. When he looked past her shoulders to see Jenny, her long dark hair falling loose around her shoulders, her smile so warm and welcoming, it was all he could do to remember how to breathe.

Her blue eyes glistened when they met his. "Such a gentleman."

"What?" he asked, so lost in her that his brain wasn't functioning at full capacity.

"The flowers."

"Oh, right, they're for you." He handed her the flowers and she sniffed them. "Daisies, my favorite. Let me guess, Garrett told you."

"Nope," he said. "You just seemed like a daisy kind of girl."

She cocked her head, and gave him a skeptical look as she narrowed her big blue eyes. "Really?"

"Really," he said. "Scout's honor."

"You were a scout?"

"I was a lot of things."

She laughed. "I bet you were." She looked at the flowers again. "You did good, Ving. These are really pretty."

"You two know I'm still here, right?" Sam cut in. When neither of them acknowledged her presence and kept staring at each other, Sam rolled her eyes. "Jesus, get a room already." She took the flowers. "These need water." She turned to leave but not before she mumbled something about them needing a good cold dousing too.

After she left, Ving let his glance move over Jenny's summery dress. "You look beautiful."

"Thank you." She looked at his khakis and dress shirt. "You clean up pretty nice yourself."

"Ready?" he asked. She nodded and he slipped his arm around her waist, anxious to get to know her better. Twenty minutes later, they sat across from each other on a blanket at the park, the sun setting in the horizon.

Ving laid out the food the neighbor's kids had helped him prepare and uncorked a bottle of wine. When he caught Jenny grinning at him, he narrowed his eyes. "What?"

She waved her hand over the food. "I didn't expect this. I figured we'd be sitting in some fancy restaurant."

"Sorry to disappoint—"

"I never said I was disappointed."

"Good. And I have a confession. It was Marley's idea." He grinned. "I think her mom lets her watch too many romantic comedies. She's going to grow up with far too many expectations," he said, chuckling.

"Marley?"

"One of the little girls I was babysitting. Marley is the oldest girl, Kate is the youngest. Andy is the one who knocked you into the pool."

"Do you babysit often?"

"Their mom is a nurse and a single mom. She's a shift worker and money is tight, so I do what I can to help out."

"That's very sweet of you."

"Not really. I actually just use them to pick up chicks. Girls dig a guy with kids, you know."

Jenny laughed. "It's puppies guys use, not children."

"Shit." He shook his head. "I always get that mixed up. I guess now I have to get a puppy."

"I'm sure Garrett can help you out with that. He and a bunch of the guys are training shelter dogs to help bomb-hunting soldiers on American soil. From what Garrett said, there are many unexploded bombs across the country left over from former training camps during the wars." He sat there listening to her, then she narrowed her eyes. "Wait you already know all this, don't you?"

"Yeah."

"And you let me go on and on anyways?"

"I like listening to you talk."

She rolled her eyes. "You talk for a while."

"Okay, well, I've signed on to help the guys. I even made a trip to the shelter this morning."

"You did?"

"Of course."

She glanced around the park, then said quietly, "You know. I think you might be too good to be true."

He pitched his voice low and sidled closer. "I can be bad," he murmured, only half teasing.

She grinned, took a sip of her wine, then exhaled slowly. "I like this. I like it a lot, Ving."

"I like you a lot," Ving said.

"You don't even know me."

"I know enough."

She pursed her lips and stared at him. "Maybe I don't."

"Okay, what do you want to know?" he asked, holding out a container of grapes to her. She popped one into her mouth and her eyes narrowed as she chewed. "What kind of name is Ving, anyway? Is it short for something?"

He laughed. "Now you sound like your roommate." He took a sip of his wine. "Speaking of your roommate, you two seem..."

"Different?"

"Yeah."

"We're not so different."

"She's full of piercings and tattoos."

Jenny gave him a wry look. "Who says I'm not?"

"I saw you in your bathing suit, remember?"

She arched a brow. "It was a one-piece."

"So you're saying I'm going to find all kind of interesting things when I see you in a two-piece?" As he visualized it a tremor moved through him, because he knew he'd find all kinds of interesting things, indeed.

"Maybe." She crossed her legs and nibbled on a piece of cheese. God, she looked so sweet and inviting it was all he could do not to lean in for a kiss. She chased the cheese with a sip of wine, then said. "Sam and I go way back. I was a teen when my father died, and I went through a rebellious stage. I hung out with the wrong people, did the wrong things. Sam was part of that crowd, and was just as lost as I was."

Ving put his hand on hers and gave a squeeze. "I'm sorry about your dad. Garrett has never talked much about him."

"We all grieve in different ways." She took another sip of wine and Ving refilled her glass. "Anyway, if it wasn't for my mom, and not giving up on Sam or me, who knows where we'd be today. She enrolled Sam in art classes, and now she makes and sells her own jewelry. It was swimming lessons for me. Now I'm a lifeguard and give lessons. I really love it."

"Your mom sounds terrific."

"She is. How about your folks? Are you close?"

"We are. They live in Tallulah, Louisiana, and I visit as much as I can. Now that I'm out of the army I'll be able to see them more."

"What did you do in the army?"

"Apache pilot."

"Really, wow, I'm impressed."

He grinned. "As you should be."

She whacked him and when he feigned hurt she rolled her eyes. "So I guess it is true."

"What true?"

"That all pilots have God complexes."

"Funny, I heard the same thing about lifeguards."

"Hey," she said, her laugh dissolving. But he wasn't sure if it was because of his teasing or the fact that he had shifted to sit beside her, their legs touching, the heat of her body messing with him in mind-fucking ways.

"This is...nice." She leaned back on her elbows and looked up at the dark sky. "I've never been on a picnic date before." She turned to face him and her hair fell over her shoulders. "You're just full of contradictions, aren't you?"

"Meaning?"

"You're just different from most guys. Like I said, I'm beginning to believe you're too good to be true."

He dropped down onto his back, rolled onto his side, and flattened his hand over her stomach. "And like I said, I can be bad. If that's what the lady wants."

She looked back up at the sky. "I...uh... It's getting late. The park will be closing soon."

He moved closer and his cock thickened against her leg. He felt a quiver move through her. "I'm not ready for this night to end, Jenny," he whispered.

She angled her head to see him, went quiet, thoughtful for a moment, then said, "Let's go."

"Where?"

"I'll only tell you if you tell me what Ving is short for."

"Forget it," he said. "The only time that will cross anyone's lips is when the priest says it on my wedding day."

"We'll see. I'll get it out of you yet."

Chapter Three

"Take a left here," Jenny said, pointing to the community center's parking lot.

Ving narrowed his eyes and shot her a confused look when he saw she was taking him to the pool. "You want to go swimming?"

"I think Sam was right. We could use a good dousing in cold water."

He laughed, and without a hint of embarrassment, adjusted his khaki shorts. "I guess you noticed how much I like you."

She looked at him, and her entire body warmed. "I like you too, Ving."

He slammed his truck into Park and turned to her. Shifting closer, he touched her hair, the backs of his fingers brushing along her cheek. His dark gaze moved over her face as he wound a loose strand around his finger. His voice dropped an octave when he said, "I'm glad to hear that."

"It's strange. I just met you, but I feel like I've known you forever." She looked out the windshield at the empty parking lot, hardly able to believe how fast she was falling for the guy. "It's all happening so quickly and to be honest, I feel like I'm skydiving without a parachute."

"Don't worry. If you fall, I'll catch you." He gave her a wink, and she guessed he was referring to her spill in the pool.

"I kind of think you would."

"I would." His glance moved over her face, and she found herself leaning in to him, craving his closeness. "Do you believe in love at first sight?" he asked.

She considered it for a moment. "No, I don't think so."

"I never used to either."

Her heart raced, loving the way this guy made her feel, and loving more how honest and open he was about everything, including his feelings. God, was he for real?

"Let's go for a swim," she said.

Ving looked around. "Isn't it closed?"

She reached for the door handle. "Yeah, but I have a key."

"Ah, so the girl can be bad too."

"I never claimed to be an angel," she said and hopped from the truck.

Ving came around to meet her. Equal amounts of heat and desire raced through her blood as he put his hand on the small of her back. She made her way to the staff lounge and fished her key from her purse. She opened the door, stepped inside and turned to him.

She sized up his body—and oh what a body it was—then pointed to the lost and found bin. "I'm sure I can find you a bathing suit that fits."

He frowned. "I'd rather go commando than let my guys hang out in someone else's shorts."

Jenny laughed. "You can't go commando, this is a public pool."

"But there's no one here to see me."

"I'll see you," she rushed out. Before he could protest, she reached in to the bin and pulled out a pair of men's shorts. "Here put these on."

"One condition."

She planted her hand on her hip. "What?"

"I get to see you in a two-piece." He reached in to the bin and pulled out the tiniest of tiny bikini bottoms.

"Those are like a children's size six."

He grinned. "I know."

"Nice try." She grabbed them and tossed them back. "I have my own two piece, thank you very much." His tortured moan reached her ears as she spun on her heels. She pulled out her string bikini from the locker in the lounge area and disappeared into the female changing room.

She peeled off her dress, fully aware of how crazy this was, how fast this was moving as she slipped into her bikini. But the truth was she liked Ving and wasn't ready for this night to be over.

When she stepped back into the lounge area, Ving stood there in his sexy boxer briefs, and she didn't miss the hard ridges straining against the cotton material.

She sucked in a breath, and said, "You didn't change."

"I think these work better."

Oh, so do I...so do I...

She grabbed two towels from her locker. "Come on then."

Keeping the lights off, they quietly walked to the pool. She dipped her toe in to check the temperature, but the next thing she knew she was in Ving's arms and he was jumping into the deep end with her.

He dragged her under and when she surfaced her breath came in a ragged burst. He laughed, but then it dissolved, his eyes locking on her mouth.

"Wait, did you take in water?" he asked.

Her heart pounded against her ribcage, her entire body reacting to his closeness. "I...I think I did," she said, knowing full well where he was going with this.

He backed her up until she was pressed against the pool wall and when she felt his hard cock against her leg, her nipples tightened painfully. "I think a little mouth-to-mouth is in order."

"Actually, I believe it's necessary," she said, faking a cough.

The second his mouth closed over hers desire twisted inside her. His hand reached around to hold the back of her neck, while his other one grabbed her leg and wrapped it around his hip.

She circled her thighs around him, needing to touch him, to stroke his hard body. She ran her fingers over his shoulders, reveling in the feel of his muscles bunching beneath her fingers.

"Jesus, Jenny. I want you so much," he murmured into her mouth, his voice hoarse, labored. "But if this is going too fast for you, tell me to slow down and I will."

"I've never gone this fast before," she said. "But I want this, Ving. I want you."

Her words seemed to unleash something in him. He deepened the kiss and pushed against her, his thick cock pressing against her pussy.

They exchanged kisses for a long time, their moans of pleasure carrying in the quiet night. His mouth moved to her neck, and his lips burned her flesh as one hand toyed with the strings on her bikini top.

He inched back and looked at her as he gave a little tug on the strings around her neck. "I like you in this suit. But I'd like you even better out of it." He untied the bow and her top fell forward, exposing her breasts.

His eyes left hers and slowly tracked down her body. The tortured look on his face as he took in her nakedness made her feel so special, so beautiful. "My God," he whispered. "I'm the luckiest man in the world to be here with you." Her heart swelled as he dipped his head and the second his hot mouth closed over her nipple, she writhed against him, her hand going around his head to hold him to her. He flicked her nipple with his tongue and she arched into him, overwhelmed with the things he made her feel.

Her head fell back against the pool as he sucked and nipped her breasts. As she looked at the star-studded sky, it occurred to her that she was feeling things she'd never felt before.

He released the remaining ties around her back and her top fell into the water. He growled, his hand moving down her side, tracing her contours, and when he removed her from his hips and stepped back, putting an inch between them, her legs straightened beneath her.

His eyes met hers and her body trembled as they exchanged a long, heated look. He stared at her for a moment longer, then touched her thighs. Her sex fluttered in response. His fingers climbed higher, rubbing her through her tiny bikini bottoms. "I'm so happy to be here with you." He pushed the fabric to the side and swiped his finger over her clit.

"Oh, God," she cried out.

"I want to make you feel really good."

"You are," she murmured, moving her hips as he continued to stroke her. "Believe me, you are."

His mouth found hers again, and he kissed her passionately as he swept the rough pad of his thumb over her clit. He groaned as she touched his body, her hands going to the huge bulge in his shorts.

"Fuck," he said when she massaged him through the material. Desperate to get him naked so she could stroke the length of him, she tugged on the band. "Jesus, Jenny," he murmured, longing coloring his voice. "Keep that up and I'll be done before I get started."

She pressed her mouth to his neck, tasting his skin as she breathed in his scent. He pushed a finger inside her and her body convulsed, a barrage of sensations rushing through her.

She began breathing harder as he pumped into her, taking her higher and higher until nothing mattered but this moment and this man.

"So good," she cried out.

"Yeah, baby," he murmured. "I want you to feel good."

He swiped his finger over the sensitive bundle of nerves inside her, and just like that she climaxed. "Oh, God," she said, her cries muffled as he pressed his lips to hers. Good Lord, she'd never orgasmed so fast before. But this man, and the way he made her feel, pushed her over the edge in record time. She gripped his arms and squeezed, riding out each glorious wave of pleasure.

When her body stopped spasming, he put his hands around her waist and anchored her to him. He carried her to the stairs and set her on the top step. With her body out of the water, he kneeled before her and gripped her bottoms. A warm quiver moved through her as he slowly dragged them down her legs.

"I want to be inside you," he whispered, his fingers stroking her inner thighs, so gentle, so intimate...so arousing.

Warmth spread over her skin as desire seared her insides. She touched his cheek, and the hard angles of his face softened when his gaze met hers. "I want that too," she said.

Just then the muscles along his jaw rippled, and he pressed his palm to his forehead. "Shit."

"What?" she asked.

"I don't have a condom."

"I'm on the pill, and I'm clean."

He threaded his fingers through her hair. "I'm clean too, Jenny." His voice dropped to a whisper and there was so much emotion on his face when he said, "Trust me when I tell you that I don't make a habit of sleeping around, and I've always used protection with the women I've been with."

"I trust you," she said, realizing that she truly did.

Her words seem to touch something in him. He ran his thumb over her cheek, then gripped her hips and gave a tug. As he spread her legs and put them around his hips, she went back on her elbows, so desperate to feel him inside her. He leaned over her and his crown breached her opening as his mouth found hers. She moved her hips, welcoming him to her body. He growled as she offered herself to him, then, in one quick thrust he pushed into her.

"Yes," she cried as he filled her completely.

He stilled inside her and took a deep, gulping breath. "You feel so good, baby. So damn good."

Her heart picked up tempo as their bodies rocked together and soon she was lost in the sensations. He kissed her deep and drew her tongue into his mouth. She moaned and pressed her breasts to his chest, craving the feel of him against her skin. He continued to pump deep, unearthing things in her that left her wanting so much more from him.

Her skin grew tight as he pounded harder, like he couldn't get deep enough, like he was chasing more than just an orgasm. His hand stroked her cheek, his touch the most intimate thing she'd ever felt. God, how had things turned so intimate so quickly? She wasn't sure, but she knew something was happening between them, something neither had any control over. She looked into his eyes and everything in the soft way he looked at her told her he felt the connection every bit as much as she did.

"Baby, you got me right there," Ving said, as he slipped a hand between their bodies to lightly stroke her clit. Soft quakes began at her core and rippled onward and outward. She drew a shaky breath as he kept her hovering on the edge.

She felt a shudder move through him and knew he was barely hanging on as he applied more pressure to her clit, clearly wanting to take her over before he let go. Who was she to disappoint him? She thrust her pelvis forward, her blood pounding hard as she took every inch of him inside her.

"That's it, sweetheart. Come for me."

She gripped his biceps, holding on to him as she let go, all thoughts slipping away as heat flamed through her. A moment later her body splintered into a million tiny pieces, her muscles clenching so hard around his cock, the world around her fading in and out of existence. A cry escaped her lips, her hot release dripping down her legs. Oh, God, the pleasure was exquisite. She closed her eyes and concentrated on the waves of ecstasy, each gripping pulse of release.

A growl ripped from Ving's lungs and she flicked her lids open to see him. One hand crushed her hair as he threw his head back and stilled inside her. Her heart fluttered, loving the way he never held anything back. He swelled inside her and she squeezed her muscles, her body trembling as she held him in tight.

They held on to each other as if their lives depended on it as they gasped for breath, both coming back down to earth slowly.

Ving was the first to break the quiet. He inched back, his fingers playing through her hair. "That was... Baby, you're amazing."

She smiled, loving the way he made her feel. "You're not so bad yourself."

They exchanged another long, heated look, then he kissed her deeply and whispered into her mouth, "I want you. All of you."

Her bikini top floated by and she grabbed it. "No strings?" she teased, twirling her bikini top around her fingers.

"All strings," he said. When she caught the seriousness in his eyes, she knew they weren't talking about her string bikini, or a no-strings-attached affair.

He drew her to him, his lips so soft, so tender as they moved over her mouth. Her heart missed a beat. The guy was all strength and muscle, yet he touched her with such tender, gentle hands.

"I can't get enough of you," he murmured.

Knowing they should probably get out of the pool, she said, "Should we go back to your place?"

"No."

"No?"

"It's too far. I want you again, right now. But this time I'm want to go slower, so I can touch and taste you all over." He scooped her up, along with their towels, and carried her inside the staff lounge. He laid her towel out on the sofa then nudged her until she fell backward. Once she was spread out on the cushions, he climbed over her, and once again she was lost in the magic of his touch. They made love well into the morning, and with the sun on the horizon, Ving touched her face.

"I'd better get you home before we get caught."

She smiled. "I supposed that wouldn't look good to management."

His gaze moved over her face. "I want to see you again."

"I want that too."

He furrowed his brow like he was in thought. "This afternoon I'll be at the compound with the dogs, and tonight I promised the kids a sleepover."

"That's okay, it's my day off and I actually told my friend, Skylar, I'd help her out at her bar tonight."

"Skylar Redmond, the owner of the Sky Bar?"

"You know her."

"Not well. I've been by there a few times, one of my best buds, Matt James, works there."

She nodded. "Yeah, I've seen him around."

"What about tomorrow?"

"I work at eight in the morning."

"I'll come by with the kids at seven thirty."

She laughed. "But I won't be here until eight."

"We'll wait."

She ran her nails over his flesh, and when he quivered, her heart squeezed. "You're a crazy man, you know that?"

"Nah, I'm just the guy who's crazy about you."

"Earth to Jenny."

Jenny spun around to face her friend, Sky. The tray Jenny was balancing in one hand nearly crashed to the floor with the quick movement. "What?" Jenny asked as Sky stared at her with curious eyes.

Sky laughed. "You're a million miles away, that's what. Want to explain?"

Jenny looked around at the patrons sitting near her, then lowered her voice, excited to tell her friend about Ving, simply because she wanted to talk, and think about him. "I've met someone."

Sky's eyes widened as she grabbed Jenny's hand to drag her behind the bar. "What? Who? When did this happen? Tell me everything." Then her friend stopped speaking, understanding backlighting her eyes as her gaze moved over Jenny's face. "Oh, my God. You had sex," she blurted out.

From the end of the table Matt James lifted his head, and Jenny put her finger over her lips to quiet her friend. "Shh," she said, unable to hold in a chuckle. "Matt will hear you."

Sky waved a dismissive hand toward Matt. "Don't worry about Matt. He's trustworthy and won't say anything."

Jenny took note of the way Matt was watching Sky, the way he always watched Sky. "Speaking of Matt, have you two ever...you know."

"No," Sky said. "We're just friends. We go way back. But never mind that, this is about you, not me and Matt."

She gave Sky a wry look. "Well, it's kind of about Matt."

Sky's eyes widened, her glance going from Jenny to Matt back to Jenny. "What, did you sleep with Matt? Why am I just finding out about this now?"

"No, no. It's not Matt."

Sky crinkled her nose and shook her head. "I don't get it, then how is it about Matt?"

She pitched her voice low, leaned in and whispered, "I slept with his best friend."

Sky opened her mouth, then closed it again, like she couldn't get the words out. Then she finally asked, "You slept with Ving?"

Jenny nodded eagerly. "Last night. I met him at the pool and we went out on a date. It all happened so fast I didn't even have time to tell you." She grabbed Sky's hand. "I'm sort of crazy about him, Sky."

The smile fell from Sky's face. "Really?"

"Yeah, why?" Jenny asked, a nervous sensation invading her gut.

Sky twirled her apron strings around her fingers, a familiar habit when she had something on her mind. "Nothing, it's just..."

"Just what?"

She brushed her bangs from her face, and rolled one shoulder. "He's really good looking, and..."

"And?" Jenny pressed.

"And, well, he's very popular with the girls, if you know what I mean." Sky looked around the bar, taking note of all the pretty girls working the room. "He's been in here a few times to see Matt since he's been back from overseas, and the girls are all over him. He's like nectar to the honey bee."

A knot tightened in Jenny's stomach and she let go of Sky's hand. "Yeah but that doesn't mean he sleeps around," she said, feeling very defensive. "He told me he didn't."

Sky let loose a slow breath. "Guys will say anything to get what they want, Jenny." She grabbed Jenny's hand and squeezed. "Look, all I'm saying is I want you to be careful. You know I love you and want you to be happy, but sometimes you can be so trusting."

It was true. She could be very trusting. But still, Ving wasn't like that, right?

Dark lashes blinked over concerned eyes. "I love that you jump into things head first, and love your enthusiasm for life, but this time I think you should take it slow, okay?"

Jenny swallowed, because *slow* didn't even begin to describe what she was doing with Ving.

"Okay," she said, even though she knew it was too late for that. Sky gave her a hug and turned her attention to the patrons at the bar. Jenny glanced around the room and her heart pounded as she thought about her night with Ving. He was so sweet, so caring, so amazing. Everything in her gut told her she could trust him. That he wasn't the kind of guy to say whatever it took to get a girl into bed.

Then again, she'd been wrong before, and she couldn't forget that he didn't want to go back to his place last night, and tonight he said he couldn't see her because he had to babysit the kids. Was it possible that he had something to hide and didn't want her there? Maybe she should have called Garrett to ask about him. But she never felt the need to because Ving seemed so honest and open in everything he did and said. She thought about calling him now, but a part of her didn't want to, because she wanted to believe in Ving.

Many hours later, after helping Sky out, Jenny made her way home. She crawled into bed, her body tired but her mind too hyped up to sleep. She thought over her conversation with Sky for the hundredth time, and after a deep consultation with herself, she decided while her friend said those things because she cared about Jenny's well-being, she was wrong where Ving was concerned. He was a great man and she could trust him. She was sure of it. With that last thought in mind, she fell asleep, anxious to see him first thing tomorrow morning.

A bird outside Jenny's window pulled her awake. She blinked her eyes open and groaned when she noticed that it was only six in the morning. She tossed and turned for half an hour, all the while thinking about Ving, and when she finally concluded that she wasn't going to fall back to sleep, she pushed her covers off.

She jumped from her bed, showered and dressed, then made her way to Sweetie's Café. Knowing Ving had said he'd be up early to meet her at the pool, she decided to surprise him and the kids with a special breakfast before they all began their day. She ordered bagels, old-fashioned donuts and croissants, and two strong coffees for her and Ving. A short while later she drove down his street, stopping when she spotted his truck. She made her way to his door, taking note of the swingset in his backyard. Why would the set be in his yard and not the neighbor's? Just as she was about to knock, the door flew open.

She came face to face with the three kids he was babysitting, and the littlest girl, Kate, looked at the bag of goodies with bright-eyed enthusiasm.

"Are those for us?" Andy asked.

"They are." She handed him the bag and looked past his shoulder, expecting to see Ving milling about. "Isn't Ving up?"

"No," Marley, the oldest girl, said. She pointed toward the hall, to where Jenny assumed the bedrooms were. "And you don't want to go in there. He's grumpy."

"Grumpy? Why is he grumpy?"

Kate rubbed her tired eyes. "Because he was up all night with Ella."

An uneasy feeling moved through Jenny as the seed of doubt Sky planted last night started blossoming inside her. "Ella?" Who the heck was Ella?

The boy reached into the bag, pulled out a croissant, then handed the bag to Marley. "Yeah, and she was so loud, she kept us up all night long."

Kate plugged her ears, like she was reliving the god-awful noise.

"No one got any sleep," Marley said, grabbing a bagel.

"He was supposed to take us to the pool," Kate said, as she pulled a treat from the bag. "But every time we go in there to get him, Ella whines so he doesn't want to leave her."

Jenny's heart raced. What the heck was going on? Why would Ving be in bed with a girl when he was babysitting three kids, and why would Ella be so loud that they could hear her?

Deciding to get to the bottom of matters, she looked at Andy and tried to keep her voice even when she said, "Why don't you take your sisters to play on the swingset while I check on things."

"Sure," he said around a mouthful of croissant.

Once they disappeared through the door, Jenny made her way down the hall. She knocked quietly, worried about what she was going to find on the other side. For a second she thought about leaving and trying to put Ving out of her mind, but she was pretty sure that wasn't possible, and she did want to get to the bottom of matters.

"Come in," he grumbled.

Jenny sucked in a breath and held it as she opened the door, and when she saw a figure in bed beside him, her blonde hair splayed across the pillow, her heart fell into her stomach.

As the image dredged up old memories, a lump pushed into her throat, and she gripped the doorframe.

"Ving," she managed to get out as her heart slammed in her chest. "What's going on?"

"Jenny," he said, surprise in his voice as he jolted upright in bed. "What are you doing here?" He pushed the covers off, and slid his legs over the side of the mattress, and that's when she got a good look at Ella.

Her pulse leapt in her throat and her knees nearly gave as she took in the vision before her. She thought about her whirlwind romance with Ving and how the night before he'd asked her if she believed in love at first sight. The truth was she didn't. At least not until she met him.

His gaze went from her to Ella, then back to her again. He gave her a sheepish look, one that had love rushing to her heart, and said, "She was sick. I think it was something she ate." He ran his hand over Ella's head, stroking softly. "She's feeling much better now though."

Jenny's whole world shifted and a bone-deep warmth flooded her as he looked at her with such warmth and emotion—such happiness to see her. God, how could she not love a man who watched his neighbor's kids, a man who put a swingset in his backyard for them because their mother likely couldn't afford it? A man who stayed up all night with a sick dog and let her sleep in his bed?

A man who said he wanted it all—with her.

She stood there looking down at him, her heart swelling with all the things she felt for him. That's when two things occurred to her. Too good to be true really did exist, and eventually she'd learn his full name, because, like he said, this romance came with strings, and someday soon she was going to be his wife.

About the Author

New York Times and *USA Today* bestselling author Cathryn Fox is a wife, mom, sister, daughter and friend. She loves dogs, sunny weather, anything chocolate (she never says no to a brownie), pizza and red wine. She has two teenagers who keep her busy with their never-ending activities, and a husband who is convinced he can turn her into a mixed-martial-arts fan. Cathryn can never find balance in her life, is always trying to find time to go to the gym, can never keep up with emails, Facebook or Twitter, and tries to write page-turning books that her readers will love.

To learn more about Cathryn please visit: cathrynfox.com.

You can find her on Facebook: facebook.com/cathrynfox

Twitter: @writercatfox

Unwrap a little holiday wickedness…

Silk
© *2013 Cathryn Fox*
Whispering Cove, Book 8

The pleasures of Christmas. Love. The two things Jon Wilson doesn't think he deserves, thanks to a holiday accident that took his parents. Under pressure from his uncle, Jon returns to Whispering Cove for the annual festivities, but he's counting down the hours until he can hop a Christmas Eve plane back to his Miami medical practice.

Chef Lila Sheppard left the big city and its fast-talking men for Whispering Cove, hoping to settle down with a nice, small-town boy. Until Mr. Picket Fence appears, though, she's not opposed to a tango on the wild side. When Jon shows up—gorgeous, hot and temporary—she figures Santa delivered her Christmas present a few days early.

Soon they're heating up cold, wintry nights, but as they get lost in each other's arms, Lila begins to realize their brief affair has become something more. Yet she wonders if there's enough magic in Whispering Cove to show Jon that love can heal all hearts…and that there's only one place he belongs.

Warning: Contains enough passion to melt ice, and turn any blustery wintry night into a hot, sultry holiday.

Available now in ebook from Samhain Publishing.

What happens on the island, lingers in the heart.

Hawaiian Holiday
© *2013 Crystal Jordan*
Destination: Desire, Book 2

Julie Simms moved back to Half Moon Bay to take over her ailing great aunt's fiber arts store, and stayed by her side until the end. Now it's Julie's first Christmas without the sassy old lady, and grief drives her to take some much-needed time off away from a town full of memories.

A week in Honolulu—hula dancers, coconut palms, and sunny beaches—is exactly what she needs, plus a bonus: meeting a gorgeous man who makes her forget everything except getting naked. With him. As often as possible.

Stanford Professor Lukas Klein, who's just finished up a conference and is ready for a break, hasn't been this intensely attracted to a woman since his divorce. He's been leery of getting too deeply involved in a relationship, yet Julie is a breath of fresh air he can't resist. And doesn't even want to try.

Half Moon Bay and Stanford aren't that far apart, but the magic of paradise could be too far removed from reality to let an attraction this mind-blowing last forever.

Warning: Crochet bikinis and sex on the beach (the drink and the real thing). Hawaiian breezes ignite an affair hot enough to reanimate a dormant volcano.

Available now in ebook and print from Samhain Publishing.

It's all about the story...

Romance

HORROR

www.samhainpublishing.com

CPSIA information can be obtained at www.ICGtesting.com
Printed in the USA
BVOW08s0316240715

410083BV00002B/71/P